the
PEACOCK
DETECTIVES

the
PEACOCK
DETECTIVES

Carly Nugent

HARPER

An Imprint of HarperCollins*Publishers*

Typography by Michelle Taormina
19 20 21 22 23 PC/LSCH 10 9 8 7 6 5 4 3 2 1
❖
First American edition, 2020
Originally published in 2018 by The Text Publishing Company, Melbourne,
Australia

For Gramps

PART ONE

Autumn

ONE

TODAY WOULD HAVE BEEN AN ORDINARY SATURDAY, except that two things happened:

1. The peacocks escaped, and
2. I started writing this story.

Dad says if you want to write a story you should start by choosing a topic that you know a lot about. That's why this isn't a story about France (which I know a little bit about but not a lot), and it isn't a story about my big sister, Diana (who I used to know a lot about but now that she is fourteen-turning-fifteen I don't anymore). This is a story about peacocks. I know a lot about peacocks because:

a) Two peacocks live with Mr. and Mrs. Hudson in the vacation houses across the road from me, and

b) I'm good at finding them when they go missing.

I'm good at finding a lot of things because I'm good at noticing details. For example, in February Mum was trying to make apple crumble and she couldn't find the cinnamon. I went through the cupboard and sniffed everything and found it in a jar labeled "Cumin." And last year when Diana lost her new bra I noticed some dirt on my dog Simon's nose, which meant that he had been digging. I found Diana's bra in a hole under the bay tree. I guess Simon doesn't like Diana being fourteen-turning-fifteen either.

Dad also says that if you want to be a writer you have to be good at details because details are what color the pictures in people's heads when they read. I keep all my details, and this story, in my Notebook for Noticing, which Dad gave me for my birthday last year. Here are some examples of the other details in my notebook:

Chard for dinner tonight ☹

Diana was on her phone for three hours today.

Dad is yawning a lot.

Mum made lamingtons.

Dad says that a story also has to have an Inciting Incident at the beginning. An Inciting Incident is something that happens to get the story started, like a problem that has to be fixed, or a mystery that has to be solved. And the Inciting Incident for this story is that the peacocks escaped and Mr. and Mrs. Hudson came over to ask me to help find them.

Noticing details makes me a good writer and it also makes me a good detective, like Sherlock Holmes. Mr. and Mrs. Hudson knew I was a good detective because I was the one who found their peacocks when they escaped the last time. I found them by noticing some peacock poo on the ground, which meant I knew which direction the peacocks had gone in, which meant I could follow them and find them behind the fire station, where they were sitting on a coiled-up hose.

"Cassie Andersen, Peacock Detective!" Dad said. I thought this sounded good, so I wrote it on a piece of cardboard and made it into a badge. Then I pinned it to the backpack Grandpa gave me for Christmas, and now everywhere I go I'm ready for solving mysteries.

The first thing I did when Mr. and Mrs. Hudson asked for my help was write down everything I already knew about the peacocks in my Notebook for Noticing:

1. There are two peacocks: William Shakespeare (who is a boy) and Virginia (who is a girl). Technically, Virginia is a peahen, not a peacock.
2. William Shakespeare and Virginia live with Mr. and Mrs. Hudson in the vacation homes across the road from my house.

3. William Shakespeare and Virginia are ornamental pets. Ornamental means decorative, like when you put baubles and little wooden Santas on your Christmas tree to make it look nice. Simon, however, is not an ornamental pet. He is a pet for doing things, like barking and sniffing and getting patted.

4. Virginia and William Shakespeare have escaped once already in February, which was when I found them on the fire hose.

5. In the wild, boy peacocks have lots of wives, but in captivity (like being decorative pets at vacation flats) they are monogamous. Monogamous means you only have one husband or wife forever. William Shakespeare is monogamous with Virginia, just like my dad is monogamous with my mum.

6. Boy peacocks start to lose their feathers at the end of summer and the start of autumn, which, since it's March, is now (if you are reading this in a country like England or America, you should know that Australian autumn starts in March).

7. Peacocks like to have a lot of space so they can roam around.

8. Peacocks poo everywhere and it is really messy.

9. Peacocks like to have baths in dirt.

10. Peacocks like to eat insects, seeds, fruit, and sometimes small snakes.

The second thing I did was interview Mr. and Mrs. Hudson because they are the people who know the peacocks best, and I thought they might be able to give me some more details. I'm going to write down my interview here in dialogue. Dad says it's important to have dialogue in a story because it helps the reader imagine how people speak and it also stops them from getting bored reading lots of long paragraphs full of lots of long sentences that feel like they go on and on and on and never end.

Dialogue, on the other hand, looks like this:

Me: Excuse me, Mr. and Mrs. Hudson, would you mind if I asked you a few questions? (Sidenote: when you are interviewing people it's important to be polite.)

Mrs. Hudson: Not at all, Cassie, go ahead.

Me: Thank you. When was—

Mum (Interrupting): Would anyone like a cup of tea?

Mrs. Hudson: That would be lovely, thank you.

Mr. Hudson: Thank you.

Me: When was—

Mum (Interrupting again): Milk? Sugar?

Mrs. Hudson: Black, please.

Mr. Hudson: Milk, no sugar.

Me: When was—

Mum (Interrupting *again*): Caramel slice?

Me: Mum!

Mum: What?

Mrs. Hudson: Not for me.

Mr. Hudson: No, thank you.

(A pause while I wait for Mum to interrupt again.)

Mum: What are you waiting for?

Me (Sighing): When was the last time you saw Virginia and William Shakespeare?

Mr. Hudson: This morning. Before breakfast.

Mrs. Hudson: We let them out into the garden. Like we always do.

Me: And after breakfast—

(Mum interrupting again by putting cups of tea and a plate of caramel slice on the table, even though no one wanted caramel slice.)

Mrs. Hudson: Thank you, Helen.

Mr. Hudson: Thank you.

Me (Continuing, despite the unwanted presence of caramel slice and my mum): And after breakfast they were gone?

Mrs. Hudson: Yes.

Mr. Hudson: They were gone.

Me: I see. (Pause while I write down important details) Is there anything else you can tell me about William Shakespeare and Virginia? Anything . . . unusual?

Mrs. Hudson: Unusual? Sebastian? (Sebastian is Mr. Hudson's first name.)

Mr. Hudson: I suppose . . .

Me (Excited because I could tell by the way they didn't finish their sentences that I was getting close to an important detail): Yes?

Mrs. Hudson: They've been a lot noisier than normal recently. Especially Virginia. But I've no idea why.

Me (Trying to hide my interest because good detectives never give away their real feelings): I think I've got enough information to start investigating. Thank you for your time, Mr. and Mrs. Hudson.

Mrs. Hudson: Thank you, Cassie.

Mr. Hudson: Thank you. And don't worry too much— I'm sure they'll find their way home eventually.

Then Mum sat down at the table and started talking to Mr. and Mrs. Hudson about the night classes she is taking, which had nothing to do with peacocks and was boring. So I got up and went to my room and added another important item to the list of things I know about the peacocks:

11. William Shakespeare and Virginia were being noisier than normal.

I felt like this was important but I didn't know exactly why. I did know, though, that when you are writing a story (or looking for peacocks) things are not always clear from the beginning. So it's important to listen to your feelings and write down everything you can.

TWO

MY ROOM IS SMALL BUT I LIKE it because it makes me feel like I am in a burrow, like a wombat or a platypus. I have lots of brown things in my room, like a brown dressing table and a brown desk and a brown bedspread. I like feeling like there is dirt all around me. Not dirty dirt, like crumbs or bits of hair that get stuck in the bathroom drain. Clean dirt, the kind that's under grass and that worms like because it's soft and spongy and warm. Sometimes when I'm in my room I feel like a worm must feel, and it is a good feeling. It is a cozy, busy, eyes-shut feeling.

I hope reading this description of my room will help you understand me better. When you write a story it's important to use lots of details, but it's also important not to use superfluous details. Superfluous means something you don't need. In a story, superfluous details are details that the reader doesn't need to know to understand the characters. For example, you don't need to spend a lot of time describing someone's shoes (even if they are really cool shoes like those sneakers that have lights on them) unless they show you something important about that person (like they want to be an athlete, or they have a lot of money).

Sometimes it's hard, though, being the writer of the story and trying to decide what you (the person reading the story) need to know and don't need to know. For example, maybe you really like dogs and you like to imagine the world in a dog sort of way, and because of this you want to know more details about Simon. (Just in case you are that sort of person: Simon is a Brittany spaniel, and he likes to eat dog food and bananas, and he is scared of storms and vacuum cleaners.)

In this story I'm going to try to give you enough details so that you can understand, but not so many that you get bored and stop reading and go to the park or the zoo instead. Here are some important details about me that you need to understand before I tell you this story:

1. My name is Cassandra, but most people call me Cassie (unless it is a Special Occasion or they are mad at me). My name comes from a Greek

myth about a princess who can see the future, but when she tells people about it they don't believe her. This is an important detail because I also know what it feels like when people don't believe you (it feels like having no friends and being told off by teachers and yelled at by your mum).

2. I have really curly hair (like my dad) that is long because if I get it cut short it goes springy and makes my head look like a triangle. I have pale skin and freckles (also like my dad) and I get sunburned really easily so I have to cover myself in sunscreen as soon as it is summer.

3. I'm eleven-turning-twelve years old and I'm in Grade Six at school, even though I can read and write at a Year Seven level. In the school readathon last year I read twenty-six books (chapter books, not picture books) and raised $72.60. Dad says I could have skipped a grade but because my school is so small the class was full.

4. I like reading stories and I like telling them, too. The other night when we were having tea I told a story about how I couldn't eat chard anymore. I couldn't eat it because the school had given all the Grade Six kids

vaccinations that made them allergic to green leafy vegetables, and if I ate chard I would break out in pus-filled scabs and die. When I told that story Diana laughed and said, "Good one," and Mum said, "If you don't finish all your dinner you won't get any dessert," and Dad said, "What about cabbage?"

5. I understand words more than anything else because when I was little, Dad would tell me stories before I went to sleep. My friend Jonas, however, knows more about facts, like why ships don't sink and what jelly is made of. He knows facts because when he was little, his dad told him scientific things. Because Jonas knows facts and I know stories, together we know almost everything.

6. The last detail you need to know about me is that I'm really, *really* afraid of snakes. It's important that you know this so that if there is ever a snake in my story you will be ready to hold your breath and stomp your feet really loud and scare it away.

THREE

WHILE I WAS IN MY ROOM WRITING, Diana opened the door without knocking and said, "What are you doing?" She was wearing jeans and a T-shirt and she was holding a book in one hand and her phone in the other.

"Getting ready to look for Virginia and William Shakespeare," I said. I had my notebook in my backpack and I was putting on my stomping shoes—which are sneakers with really thick soles—because it was only early autumn and there might still be snakes around. "Want to come?"

Diana twisted her face into a shape that looked a bit like a question mark. Now that Diana is fourteen-turning-fifteen she is sometimes confused about what she likes to do. For example, when she was thirteen she really liked playing Hide-and-Seek, but now that she's fourteen she only plays it at birthday parties, and when she's fifteen she probably won't play it at all. So when I asked her about the peacocks I wasn't sure which direction she was going to go in—the thirteen direction or the fifteen direction.

"We can share my Saturday treat," I added. Every Saturday, after I help with shopping, Mum buys me a treat. Today I got a Wizz Fizz, which is Diana's favorite. I took it out of my bag and ripped off the top.

"Okay," Diana said.

So we went together. Diana was holding her book and her phone and the Wizz Fizz, and I was holding Simon's lead (Simon is sometimes good at sniffing out peacocks, although most of the time he gets distracted by things like long grass and pinecones).

"Is that a good story?" I asked, pointing to her book. We were walking across the road to the vacation houses, where the peacocks were last seen.

"It's not a story," Diana said. "It's about Buddhism. Aunt Sally gave it to me for Christmas."

Aunt Sally is my dad's sister who lives in The City. She has three kids (two of them are so small that they still pick their noses and eat it) and we go to her house for Christmas every year.

"What's Buddhism?" I said. Simon was pulling my

arm really hard, trying to reach a puddle.

"It's a religion," Diana said.

"Like church?" I said.

"No," Diana said. "Not like church." She said it in the voice she uses a lot now that she is fourteen-turning-fifteen. It is her you-don't-understand voice.

We were at the vacation houses by then, and we went into the garden where Mr. and Mrs. Hudson keep the peacock cage. It is a big enough cage for sleeping and sitting in, but not for walking or roaming. The cage was open because the peacocks only stayed in there at night, and in the daytime they were allowed out to roam around the garden. I bent over so I was peacock-size and went in. Diana didn't.

The cage was mostly empty. There was some brown grass on the ground, and some branches high up for the peacocks to roost (roost is a bird-word for rest) on at night, and some peacock poo, which Simon ate a bit of before I could stop him. And right at the back, stuck in the wire, was one of William Shakespeare's feathers. I knew it was William Shakespeare's feather and not Virginia's because it was big and green/blue and had a shape like an eye in the middle of it, which is the kind of feather boy peacocks have but girls don't. When a boy peacock puts all of his tail feathers up it feels like hundreds of eyes are looking at you. I pulled the feather out of the wire and put it in my backpack.

I was about to wrap up the cage part of my investigation and I turned myself around in my bent-over peacock shape to leave. Then I saw the ground from a different angle, and that was when I noticed something. In the corner of the cage some of the dirt was scraped away. It looked like the peacocks had been trying to make a hole, except the ground was too hard and all they could do was make a sort of dent. I looked closer, and got out my notebook.

"What is it?" Diana said, peering through the wire.

"Something," I said, because I didn't know how else to describe it.

Diana sighed and looked at her phone, which was beeping. I ignored her and wrote the something down.

FOUR

AFTER I HAD CLIMBED OUT OF THE peacock cage and Simon had finished peeing on the side of it Diana said, "Now what?"

"Now," I said, "we follow the poo." I pointed to a pile of soft brown peacock droppings next to Diana's boots (since Diana became fourteen-turning-fifteen she wears Doc Martens instead of sneakers).

Simon sniffed the pile, ate some of it, and veered off in the direction of a large pinecone.

Behind my house there is a river, and a small track alongside it, and a lot of bush. Because peacocks like to roam I thought the bush, which is big and perfect for roaming in, might be a good place to start looking for Virginia and William Shakespeare. Simon also likes roaming in the bush, mostly because there are lots of things to sniff. I followed Simon, and Diana followed me, and together we all went into the bush.

Dad says that when you describe an important setting in a story you should use the Five Senses to make a clear picture for the reader's brain. The Five Senses are Sight, Sound, Smell, Taste, and Touch/Temperature. Looking for the peacocks by the river in autumn is a very important setting in my story, so I hope this helps you see it clearly:

Sight

Autumn by the river looks like fat leaves and thin leaves. Some of them are still green, and some are a bit green and a bit yellow, or orange, or red. There are all different kinds of red: there is red like fire, and red like an English bus, and red like those pencils that are not quite red and not quite pink. And some leaves are brown, but not brown like a tree—they are brown like a worm, or the tummy of a bird. And when the leaves start to fall off the trees the ground is colored, too, and it looks like the world is a room with matching wallpaper and carpet.

Sound

Autumn by the river sounds like walking through crunchy leaves, and sometimes swishing through slippery leaves that are thin and soft. Sometimes it sounds like kookaburras laughing, or magpies singing. And sometimes it sounds like Diana's phone dinging with a message from Tom Golding, who is a boy who is her friend but not her boyfriend.

Smell

Autumn by the river smells like smoke. I think this is because people somewhere are burning leaves or sticks, because autumn is a safe time for burning and not a bush-fire time, like summer.

Taste

Autumn by the river tastes like fresh, damp air. Sometimes it tastes like wet leaves. And sometimes on Saturdays it tastes like Wizz Fizz.

Touch

Autumn by the river feels slippery, and almost-but-not-quite cold. It sometimes feels dark, too, because in autumn we put the clocks back, so when it's five o'clock it's really six o'clock, and there's less daylight. It's the reverse of daylight savings. It is daylight spendings.

As Simon followed his nose onto the bush track I followed him (happily) and Diana followed me (not so happily). I could tell Diana wasn't happy because she was sighing a lot and stomping her boots. Boot stomping is good for scaring away snakes, but Diana isn't scared of snakes so I knew that wasn't why she was doing it. Now that Diana is fourteen-turning-fifteen there are a lot of things I don't understand about her. Here is a list of the things I do know:

1. Diana has straight hair, and skin that tans when she goes in the sun and doesn't freckle at all. Everyone always says that Diana looks like Mum, and they are right.

2. Diana is in Year Nine, which is secondary school, and she learns things like literature and algebra.

3. She smokes cigarettes sometimes. Mum and Dad don't know this, but I do, because I'm good at noticing details, and sometimes I notice Diana smells of cigarette smoke mixed with too-much-deodorant.

4. Lots of people like Diana. I think this is partly because she is pretty and smart but mostly because she doesn't care if people like her or not.

But the list of things I don't understand about Diana is much longer than the list of things I do know. For example, I don't understand why she seems unhappy when we're walking through the bush looking for peacocks. And not being able to understand my sister, even when she is stomping along right behind me, makes me feel like I'm a million miles away from her.

FIVE

WHILE WE WERE WALKING (ME) AND SNIFFING (Simon) and stomping and texting (Diana), I tried to think of something nice to talk about that would lighten the mood, i.e. (i.e. stands for *id est* which is Latin and means "in other words") something that would cheer Diana up.

Whenever I'm feeling sad I think about the best-thing-that-has-happened-in-my-life-so-far. The best-thing-that-has-happened-in-my-life-so-far is when we went to the beach on a Family Holiday. Last year Mum and Dad and Diana and I went to Queensland. We stayed on the four-teenth floor of a big hotel and our room had a balcony and windows that went all the way down to the floor so you could always see the ocean. And every day we went swimming and every night we ate in restaurants and played Scrabble. And Diana played sharks and dolphins with me in the pool, and Dad made jokes like "Why did the sand blush? Because the sea weed," and Mum held Dad's hand and smiled.

Remembering the Family Holiday made me feel happy and I thought saying it out loud might make Diana happy, too. So, while we were stopped for Simon to sniff and pee in some long grass, I said, "Remember how in Queensland we found that thing on the beach? And we thought it was a giant shark's tooth, but Mum said it was a cuttlefish bone?"

"Yeah," said Diana, looking at her phone.

"And remember how—in Queensland—Dad ate so much Mexican food that Mum said he would turn into a taco?"

"Yeah," said Diana, typing something.

"And remember how it was sunny every single day, and it never rained?"

"Yeah," said Diana, still typing.

"And remember how we had ice cream, and we saw a pelican, and Mum and Dad held hands on the beach?"

Diana didn't say anything then, but she did look at me. Simon had finished sniffing and peeing, and he was looking at me, too.

"What?" I said.

"You shouldn't lie like that, Cassie," Diana said, in a quiet voice. "It's not funny."

"But I'm not lying!" I said, because I wasn't. Cross my heart. I started to feel that hot feeling behind my eyes that means tears are growing there.

"Whatever," Diana said. "We're not going to Queensland again, you know."

I didn't say anything.

"I'm going home," Diana finally said, and then she turned around and started walking. When I saw her from behind, she looked much more like fifteen than fourteen. And even though I didn't know why Diana was angry with me I did know—because of the way she hugged her Buddhism book against her chest and stomped her Doc Martens up the hill—she wasn't coming back.

Simon and I kept walking because we didn't know what else to do, and also because there were still peacocks to find. We walked for a long time in the bush-quiet, which is like ordinary quiet except with trees rustling and kookaburras calling and river-water running. I wished there was a switch to turn my brain off because the whole time we were walking I was thinking about Diana and her stomping boots and her Buddhism. I wished I was like Simon and could only think about what I was sniffing. But I wasn't, and I couldn't.

People always tell me I'm lying. It's unfair because—most of the time—I'm not. For example, one weekend I couldn't finish my times tables homework because there were new people moving in next door. I was pretty sure they were exotic animal smugglers so I had to investigate (it turned out that they just had a pet iguana). And when I told Mrs. Atkinson at school on Monday she said, "Don't lie, Cassie," and made me write out my eight *and* nine times tables, even though everyone else only had to write their eights. And another time when Mum asked me to help her pull out the weeds in the backyard I explained that I couldn't because there were fairies living under the rosebushes that needed those weeds for spells. Mum said, "That's not true, Cassie," and gave me the gardening gloves.

Even Dad sometimes thinks I'm lying. Like when I got a C-minus on my history project because the night before it was due a witch came to me in my sleep and told me she had hidden some treasure in the sandpit. She also said that if I didn't find it before the full moon (which was the next day) it would disappear.

"Come on, Cassandra," Dad said. He took off his glasses and rubbed the part of his face where his nose becomes his forehead.

"Really!" I said. "I had to dig all afternoon, and—"

"Stop it." Dad interrupted me before I could tell him

that I *had* found treasure in the sandpit: a pink bead necklace that I had lost two years ago, and an expensive-looking screwdriver. "That's not the truth and you know it," he said.

"But it *is*!" I said, because it was. "Cross my heart. I *did* see a witch, and the next night it *was* a full moon, and—"

"No." There was something deep in Dad's voice that made me be quiet. "The truth is that you were lazy." Dad leaned forward so that he was looking right into my eyes, like he was trying to peer inside my brain. "Isn't it?"

After Dad said that, I went to my room and pretended I was a wombat, burrowing deep under the ground. I wasn't lying, but still I had this heaviness in my stomach that wouldn't go away. And I couldn't understand why the person I love most in the world would want to make me feel that way.

SIX

ONE OF THE MOST IMPORTANT CHARACTERS IN this story is my dad. I wouldn't be able to write this story without him. My dad knows more about books and writing than anyone else I know.

My dad teaches English and English literature (which is like English, except the books are harder to learn about). He loves reading books and then talking about them, especially with me. He doesn't talk about which character was his favorite or which bit he thought was the best. Instead he talks about Themes, which are ideas that books have in them. Dad says Themes are what books are really about. I don't know how Dad finds Themes, because when I read books I just find characters and things that happen to characters. Dad says I have to look-beneath-the-surface, but when I look-beneath-the-surface of my books I just see my hands.

"What about Huck Finn," Dad asked me once. "What do you think that book's about?"

"It's about a boy called Huck," I said, "having adventures with a man called Jim."

"Yes," Dad said. "But it's really about freedom, and escaping from society."

"Is it?" I said. "Which chapter?"

Dad just smiled and told me a story about when he and Mum were at university together and they made posters and went to something called a rally and Dad got arrested for yelling a word at a policeman that I'm not allowed to say until I'm older.

I'm not sure if my story will have Themes in it. I don't know if I have to write them or if they will just get in by themselves or if the people reading this will put them in. Dad says not to worry and that when I'm older I will understand. But I still do worry, a bit.

About half the time my dad is a serious sort of dad, the kind that puts on glasses and marks essays and wants to be left alone. And about half the time my dad is a fun sort of dad, the kind that tells jokes and ruffles my hair and takes Simon for walks and gives me books to read. My dad used to write stories of his own, but then he became a teacher and had children and got a mortgage and now he says he doesn't have time to write. He says that's okay and that he wouldn't want to change me and Mum and Diana for all the books in the world. But he gets some wrinkles in his forehead when he says this, and I think that somewhere deep down in him he really does still want to write stories. And I think it makes that place deep down a little bit happier when he helps me write mine.

SEVEN

SIMON AND I SEARCHED FOR THE REST of Saturday, but we didn't find any more peacock clues. I wanted to get started again in the morning, but today was Sunday, and we had to go to church. "We" includes me, Mum and Dad, but not Diana. Because Diana is fourteen-turning-fifteen this year she has started making her own decisions. One of the decisions she made is not to go to church anymore. When I asked her why, she rolled her eyes and said, "You wouldn't understand." Then she went into her room with her phone so she could talk to Tom Golding.

I think I probably would understand because I under-stand a lot of things, like Japanese and *The Adventures of Huckleberry Finn* and what a simile is (a sentence that describes something by comparing it to something else. For example: fourteen-turning-fifteen Diana is as annoying as March flies).

When Diana decided she wasn't going to church, Mum said, "Oh? Why's that?"

"It's not for me," Diana said.

"Fair enough," Mum said.

I didn't know you could choose whether church was for you or not. I thought it was for everyone, like brushing your teeth or sleeping.

Dad was in the car waiting for Mum and me to hurry up. We got in, and that was when I spotted William Shakespeare. He was standing on our roof, playing hard to get. Another thing I know about peacocks is that they are clever—especially William Shakespeare and Virginia. For example, they know when they are in danger of being caught, and when they aren't. And right then, William Shakespeare knew that I was stuck and he was safe.

Mum and Dad didn't see him. They were too busy talking about Diana.

"She's not coming, then?" said Dad.

"She's old enough to make her own decisions," said Mum. Her face looked like a full stop.

When Dad started the car Diana was still wearing her pajamas, and William Shakespeare was still on our roof. It didn't feel right to leave them both behind like that.

As we backed down the driveway William Shakespeare called out in his sad/happy peacock voice. It sounded like he was saying "Come back!" but I don't speak peacock, so he might have been saying "Good riddance."

Church without Diana was like a number seven without a line across the middle: still a number seven, but not as much fun to write. There was no one to elbow when Miss Watson wiggled her hips around during the hymns, and when it was time for Sunday school I had to walk down the aisle and out the back on my own. Grandpa wasn't at church either, which was weird because Grandpa goes to church every-Sunday-always. I asked Mum where he was, but she shushed me because Miss Watson was doing the sermon. It made me sad that Grandpa wasn't there because the best thing to do at church is sit next to him when he sings his favorite hymn (which is "All Things Bright and Beautiful") and feel his voice vibrate all the way down from his throat to the chair and from the chair into me. And Jonas isn't ever at church because his parents are atheists, which means they believe in science instead of God.

In Sunday school Miss Robinson told us The Creation Story, which we all knew already but I didn't mind hearing again. In The Creation Story, Miss Robinson said, first there is nothing, and she used a piece of black paper to symbolize this. A symbol is a thing that is easy to see that stands for something that is hard to see. For example, it is hard to see love, but it is easy to see my dad, so my dad is a symbol for love. And William Shakespeare's feather is a symbol for the missing peacocks, since the feather is easy to see, but the peacocks—unless they are standing on my roof—are not. But symbols are not the same for everyone. When I told Jonas about my symbol for love he didn't understand. He said his symbol for love is the internet.

So the black paper was a symbol for nothing. And then out of nothing God made everything, including the planets and grass and caterpillars (Miss Robinson used colored stickers to symbolize those). And then, after six days, God had a rest. Miss Robinson didn't have anything to symbolize this—she just said it, which I thought was a bit unfair because it was hard to imagine God resting.

I think The Creation Story is a good story but Jonas doesn't. Jonas says The Creation Story is not good because it isn't true. He says the true story is that there was a big explosion in space that threw a lot of stuff around and then the Earth and the planets slowly happened. He says grass and caterpillars weren't just there after six days because they had to evolve, which means they came out of other, older things like algae and prawns. Jonas says that the algae and prawns kept getting better and better until they became grass and caterpillars. And today grass and caterpillars are still getting better but they're doing it so slowly that we don't notice it, and one day they won't be grass and caterpillars anymore but something else that we can't even imagine.

When Jonas told me this I thought it was interesting and true, but I also thought there was something missing from it, like a Main Character and an ending. Which is why even though I like Jonas's story, I still like The Creation Story, too. So when Robert Radley said Miss Robinson was lying in Sunday school this morning I told him to shut up. I felt bad for Miss Robinson because people tell me I'm lying all the time, but I'm not.

"Cassandra," said Miss Robinson in an I'm-warning-you sort of voice but with a thank-you sort of face. Then Sunday school was over and we could go, and I didn't have to say sorry to Robert Radley, which was a good thing because saying sorry to Robert Radley really would have been a lie.

EIGHT

WHEN WE GOT HOME FROM CHURCH, WILLIAM Shakespeare wasn't on our roof anymore, so Simon and I (and not Diana) went for a Sunday walk to look for him. On the way, my feet and Simon's nose led us to Grandpa's house, which is small and yellow and wooden and has a back door you can walk to from the river. I knew Simon wanted biscuits (because Simon always wants biscuits) and I wanted lemonade, and to see Grandpa since I had missed him at church, so together we decided to stop for a visit.

We found Grandpa in the backyard. He was sitting on a lawn chair doing the Sunday crossword.

"Hello, Cassie Jane," he said. Grandpa is the only person who can call me Cassie Jane. This is a compromise I have made, because I really don't like my middle name, but I really do like Grandpa. Simon ran over and started licking the back of Grandpa's hand. Grandpa gave him a pat and said, "Seven down. Nine letters, second letter i. Hard, if lift cud." He tapped the newspaper with the end of his pen. "Any ideas?"

Grandpa doesn't do normal crosswords, like other people. He does cryptic crosswords. Cryptic crosswords are crosswords where the clues don't mean what they seem to mean. For example, the clue "Hard, if lift cud" doesn't actually have anything to do with cows eating, but cows eating is what your brain automatically wants to think about when it hears the word "cud." When you do cryptic crosswords you have to make your brain think in a different way. In a way that sees how words are made, and not what they stand for.

When Grandpa said "Hard, if lift cud" I couldn't get my brain to change its thinking. This was because I was still worried about things like Diana stomping off on me, and Robert Radley saying Miss Robinson was lying. So I shook my head. Grandpa put down the paper. "Well," he said. "Time for a break anyway, I think. Lemonade?"

Simon and I followed Grandpa inside. (Simon is an outside dog at our house, but at Grandpa's he is an inside and an outside dog. He is an everywhere dog.) Grandpa's kitchen isn't very big, but it's very cozy. On his fridge, he has stick-people drawings that Diana and I did for him when we were little, and framed family photos of us when we were babies and of Mum and Dad at their wedding. He also has photos of the kids he sponsors in other countries, and letters they have written him about what they are learning at school and what their hobbies are.

Grandpa is like my dad in looks—he is also tall, and he used to have curly hair before he went bald—but not really in personality. Instead of reading, Grandpa likes to weed the garden or tinker with the car. He is always busy, and loves talking to other people, and planning things to do. I've never seen him quiet and sad and lost inside himself, the way Dad is sometimes.

When Grandpa had finished boiling water for his cup of tea and pouring my cup of lemonade, we went back outside. I carried the biscuits on a plate. Grandpa likes to feed the birds while he has afternoon tea, and as soon as we sat down two sparrows hopped over to us.

"Good afternoon, George, Mildred," Grandpa said, and threw them each a crumb of Scotch Finger. Then he took a sip of his tea. "Now, Cassie Jane," he said. "What story have you got to tell me?"

I thought for a minute, and then I started. I always tell Grandpa stories, and this time I told him a story about a family of kangaroos that lived in the bush. The little kangaroos played together every day—they played

Hide-and-Seek and Chasey and Blind Man's Bluff. Their favorite game was Scavenger Hunt, where they had to work as a team to find a list of things hidden in the bush, like red berries and pinecones and wombat poo. But then one day the oldest kangaroo said she didn't want to play anymore.

"She just hopped off by herself," I told Grandpa. "Down a different track. And left all her brothers and sisters behind."

Grandpa was looking at me carefully. Grandpa is the best at listening to stories. When he listens his eyes focus totally on you, and you know he isn't thinking about what to cook for dinner or what's on TV later. His eyes are almost better at listening than his ears.

"Is that the end?" he asked.

I shrugged. "I guess," I said. I couldn't think of another way to finish the story, even though I knew it wasn't a great ending.

"Why did the older kangaroo leave her little brothers and sisters behind like that?" Grandpa said.

"I don't know." I gave Simon half of my Monte Carlo. "Probably because she's mean."

Grandpa smiled. "You're a better storyteller than that, Cassie Jane," he said. "I bet there's another reason."

"Maybe," I said. "But I don't know what it is."

"You'll figure it out," Grandpa said. "Don't worry."

He passed me the biscuits. "Here, have a Tim Tam."

I picked up a biscuit and bit into it. When I was halfway through chewing I thought of the answer.

"Difficult," I said.

"What's difficult?" Grandpa said, with his eyebrows scrunched together.

"Seven down," I said. "It's an anagram"—(an anagram is when you mix up the letters of one word or phrase to make another word or phrase)—"If lift cud. Difficult."

Grandpa smiled and picked up the crossword and his pen. "Nice work, Cassie Jane," he said, and wrote the answer in. "See? I knew you'd figure it out."

NINE

AFTER WE LEFT GRANDPA'S HOUSE, SIMON AND I kept walking and looking for peacocks. We walked for so long that we got to the bridge, which is where the track meets the road and crosses the river. Mum says I'm not allowed to go over the bridge by myself, because over the bridge is The Other Side of Town.

I asked Jonas one day how big our town is, because he is much better at numbers than I am, and he said it is about two-thousand-people-size, which means it is a small town. Two thousand sounds like a lot to me. Two thousand pencils on a desk would be a lot of pencils, and two thousand birds in a tree would be a lot of birds. But I guess the two thousand people in our town are never all in the same place at once. If you walk down the main street you will probably only see about thirty people, and about half of those people will say hello to you because they have seen you in the school play or they know your mum from night classes or your grandpa from church. And that's what, I think, really makes it a small town.

The name of my town is Bloomsbury. I have lived in Bloomsbury for as long as I can remember. I went to kindergarten here, and not many people can remember before kindergarten. (Jonas is the only person I know who can remember being a baby. He remembers being in a cot and crying for ages and nobody coming to pick him up.) Diana can remember before we came to Bloomsbury because she was in Grade Two then. She says we used to live in The City but we moved because Mum and Dad were sick of the traffic and the noise and the prices.

My town isn't big enough to have a lot of traffic but it is big enough to have two sides. Some of the things on My Side of Town are:

1. My house
2. Jonas's house
3. Grandpa's house
4. School
5. Church
6. The post office
7. The fish-and-chip shop

And some of the things on The Other Side of
    Town are:
1. The bank
2. The Very Nice Restaurant
3. The hospital
4. The bus station
5. Lee Street (a dead-end street that Diana and
    I aren't allowed to go down because, Mum says,
    "It's just not the kind of place you need to be
    hanging around." Whenever adults talk about
    Lee Street they get this look on their faces
    like someone has just died and they are very,
    very sorry.)

At the bridge, I was about to turn around and head
home when Simon stopped and sniffed the air. I looked
up and saw what Simon was sniffing at. There, standing
right in the middle of the bridge, was Virginia.

Virginia isn't as beautiful as William Shakespeare—
her feathers are short and mostly brown and they don't
have eyes on them—but she is faster. Simon and I chased
her, but Virginia is so fast that while we were running
I couldn't think about anything except moving my legs.
We chased her right across to The Other Side of Town—
past The Very Nice Restaurant and the bank and the bus
station—and the whole time I didn't think about Diana
or Buddhism or not going on Family Holiday even once.

The whole time my brain only had one thought and that thought was *run*.

We chased Virginia all the way to the hospital. Next door to the hospital there is a small house with a fence all the way around it. Virginia flapped over the fence and behind the house and then we couldn't chase her anymore, so we stopped. Simon was panting and I had a stitch, and for a minute my only thought was *ouch*. But then—when my stitch started to undo itself—I realized that the house wasn't really a house at all. It was The Clinic.

Adults never say The Clinic in normal voices—they always whisper it or say it really fast like they want to get the words out before anybody notices. The Clinic is like a hospital, but for your brain instead of your body. I don't know what doctors do in there—like if they use stethoscopes or tongue-sticks like regular doctors. But I do know that sometimes after people start going to The Clinic the doctors send them somewhere else. And after people go somewhere else they don't always come back. I know this because Rhea Grimm (who is the tallest, meanest girl in Year Eight) used to have a dad. He used to do normal dad things, like buy the paper and drive a car and have coffee. I didn't really know him, but Bloomsbury is a small town, so I used to see him around. Then one day he stopped doing dad things and started going to The Clinic. And a few weeks after that he stopped going to The Clinic and was just gone. I never see him around anymore.

Simon sniffed and pulled on his lead to interrupt my thoughts and make me walk around the side of the fence. When I did we saw Virginia sitting in the top of a tall tree where the leaves were starting to turn brown. Simon barked and Virginia cried in her peacock way and something inside me sagged a little, like an old basketball. I was sagging partly because I knew we wouldn't be able to make Virginia come down, but also partly because of a feeling I got from looking at The Clinic that I don't know how to put into words.

TEN

WHEN WE GOT HOME ON SUNDAY AFTERNOON, I went straight across the road to tell Mr. and Mrs. Hudson about Virginia.

"Don't worry, Cassie," said Mrs. Hudson. "She'll come home when she's ready."

"Want a chocolate biscuit?" said Mr. Hudson. "I just took them out of the oven." It was nearly dinnertime, and if Mum had been there, she would have made me say "No, thank you." But she wasn't, so she couldn't, so I took one and said, "Yes, thank you," instead.

Today was Monday, which meant school, which meant I couldn't look for the peacocks. I walked to school with Diana, except I didn't really walk with her because she was walking with Tom Golding and together they were slower than snails. I like Tom Golding (because he always smiles and says "Hi, Cassie" and "See ya, Cassie"), but I don't know much about him (because he doesn't say anything else to me and because even though Diana is always talking *to* him she never talks *about* him).

Diana is in secondary school and I'm still in primary but we both go to the same place. This is because my town is small and only has enough kids for one school. The downhill part of the school is primary, and the uphill part is secondary. There isn't a fence or anything between the two halves, but everybody knows that secondary starts at the handball courts. Only secondary kids play on the handball courts, and if you're in primary the only times you can go past them are when you're doing lunch orders or walking to the oval for PE.

At little recess on Monday I went to sit near Jonas on The Snake Stairs. I used to sit with some of the Grade Six girls but they didn't like it when I told them how I had seen a UFO, or that my aunt Sally can read minds. One day when I went to sit with them they all ran into the fort and didn't come out. It took me a while to figure out that they were superheroes and had turned invisible so they could go save the world. Once I came up with that story I didn't feel so sad about not sitting with them anymore.

The stairs where I sit for lunch now are called The

Snake Stairs because one day last summer Miss Shilling came out of the back of the art room to wash the paint trays and saw a tiger snake go under the steps. Mr. Bennett (our school principal) called the council to find it, but they couldn't, so instead they put up signs near the steps that say:

DANGER! SNAKE!

And now Jonas is the only kid brave enough to sit there. Jonas isn't scared of snakes. He saw one once near the river behind his house. When I asked him what he did, he said, "Nothing." He just stood there, and then the snake slid away. This story was interesting to me because before that I had never thought that doing nothing might be the best way to deal with something.

But because I'm so afraid of snakes, I can't sit on the stairs with Jonas, so I sit on the footpath across the grass from him and we yell to each other. That Monday morning I yelled at Jonas, "What's Buddhism?"

I thought Jonas might know something about Buddhism. Jonas has his own computer in his room and the internet, which is why he knows so many facts and is always saying "Did you know?" Another reason Jonas knows so many facts is because his parents take him on holidays to places like Cambodia and the Mediterranean, where they go to museums and art galleries and jungles. For example, next week Jonas's parents are taking him on a big overseas holiday to Europe, so he can collect even more facts about France and viaducts and pizza.

Jonas knows interesting facts about everything, but his favorite facts are about sharks. He knows more about sharks than anything else. He has shark stickers on his books and on his schoolbag. He has a shark hat, a shark pencil case, and shark shoelaces. He knows so much about sharks that sometimes I wonder if he secretly is one.

A lot of kids think Jonas's facts are annoying, but I think they're interesting, which is why I asked him about Buddhism.

"It's a religion," Jonas yelled back. "From India."

"But what does it *do*?" I peeled my banana.

"It doesn't do anything," Jonas yelled. His glasses started falling down his nose and he pushed them back up. Jonas wears glasses even though he doesn't really need to, because he thinks they make him look like Stephen Hawking, who is his favorite scientist.

"But church is a religion and it does things," I yelled back. "It prays, and it sings, and it passes the collection plate."

"Buddhism's not like that. Buddhism's about thinking, and thinking isn't doing."

"Yes it is! Thinking is a verb!" I was right, but Jonas doesn't like to be wrong.

"Yeah. But," Jonas yelled (quietly).

"Yeah, but what?" I yelled (loudly).

Jonas was chewing his Vegemite sandwich extra slow. I knew he was waiting for the bell to ring, so he wouldn't have to keep having a conversation where he was wrong. Jonas is clever like that.

Jonas and I are opposites. I know a lot about reading and writing and stories, and he knows a lot about science and math and facts. Some kinds of opposites don't go together very well (like ovens and ice cream, or dogs and cats), but some kinds of opposites do (like knobbly jigsaw pieces and holey jigsaw pieces, or sweet and sour). Jonas and I are the good kind of opposite, and that's the first reason we are friends. The second reason we are friends is because Jonas is eleven-turning-twelve (like me) and he can read at a Year Seven level (like me). The third reason is because both of our dads are secondary-school teachers (my dad teaches English and Jonas's dad teaches science) and so sometimes they visit each other on weekends and after school. Jonas doesn't call his dad "Dad," though— he calls him Peter, and he calls his mum Irene. This feels right in one way, because those are their names. But it also feels not-right in another way, because usually kids call their mums and dads Mum and Dad.

And the final reason Jonas and I are friends is because

last year Jonas came to my birthday party. It was a dress-up party and Jonas's costume was Neptune, who is the God of the Sea. He had a wand shaped like a bolt of lightning and some green crepe paper that looked like seaweed around his head. We ate cake and chips and danced outside until it got dark. It was the best birthday I've ever had, which is a big thing to say, since I had already had ten birthdays in my life. But that was the only one so far where I've danced outside at night with the God of the Sea.

Because Jonas is my friend, I decided to change the subject to save him from not-knowing more about Buddhism. So I took William Shakespeare's feather out of my bag and showed it to him.

"Cool," Jonas yelled.

"Do you want to help me look for some peacocks?" I yelled. This was not something I had ever asked Jonas before, but I had a feeling he would say yes.

"Okay," Jonas yelled back.

And then the bell rang, and little recess was over, and Jonas was a Peacock Detective, and this story could keep going.

ELEVEN

MOST SCHOOL DAYS ARE NORMAL. YOU HANG up your bag, do a grammar worksheet, make a poster, eat lunch, and so on. Some school days are abnormal in a good way, like when Mrs. Atkinson gets out the gymnastics equipment, or there's a fire drill. But some school days are abnormal in an extraordinarily horrible way, like seeing Claudia Finch cry because her cat got run over. Today was one of those kinds of days.

After little recess was math, which is my least-favorite subject, which is why I was happy when Mrs. Atkinson chose me and Jonas to pick up the lunch orders from the cafeteria.

There is a good side and a bad side to doing lunch

orders. The good side is skipping fifteen minutes of math. The bad side is that, because the cafeteria is in the secondary school, getting lunch orders is risky. Usually at lunch-order-collection time all the secondary kids are in class, but every now and then some of them are wandering around. If a secondary kid is wandering around during class time it is probably because they got sent out by their teacher for chewing gum or swearing or playing with the fire extinguisher. This is the kind of secondary kid you want to avoid the most. So picking up the lunch orders can be a bit like walking through a jungle: you probably won't see any animals, but if you do chances are they will be dangerous ones.

We were almost at the handball courts when Jonas got a bloody nose. Jonas is always getting bloody noses. He has at least one bloody nose every two weeks, and even more in summer. Other kids tease him and say it's because he picks his nose, but I know that's not true, because Jonas told me once about how many germs are on your fingers and how easy it is for those germs to jump from your fingers into your nose, and then from your nose into your brain. Jonas gets bloody noses when he has to do things that are uncomfortable, like going across the handball courts into the secondary school where there are kids who call him Frog Eyes and Nerd Boy. Today Jonas had an especially bad bloody nose—so bad he couldn't talk because he had to hold both hands over his face. And when he ran off in the direction of the nurse's office I knew I was on my own.

I crossed the handball courts, and the jungle on the other side was quiet. All the secondary kids were tucked safely in their classrooms. I made it past the secondary lockers and the secondary art room. The mums working in the canteen smiled at me when I knocked at the back door.

"All on your own today?" said a mum with brown hair in a ponytail. I nodded. "Are you all right to carry this?"

She gave me the plastic lunch-order tub filled with pies and sausage rolls in brown paper bags. It was heavy and left me without any free hands, but I could carry it. I gave her a confident smile, and she gave me a Caramello Koala to say thank you.

I was feeling much braver on my way back with the Caramello Koala in my pocket and the hot pastry smell wafting up into my face. I thought that this might be how Simon feels when he is sniffing and walking and not-thinking. I even slowed down so I could miss a bit more math. I walked past the secondary art room and some of the secondary lockers. I was almost at the handball courts.

And that was when I saw her.

She was going in the direction of Mr. Bennett's office,

but she was dawdling. She scuffed her feet and stopped every four or five steps to look at something on the ground or pick at her fingernails.

Rhea Grimm.

Here are all the things I know about Rhea Grimm:

1. She is in Year Eight.
2. She does horrible things to teachers, like prank-calling them and putting nail polish remover in their coffee.
3. She gets sent to the office a lot.
4. Her dad used to go to The Clinic. Now he's just gone.
5. She is really mean to kids who are younger than her (i.e. me).

As soon as I saw Rhea Grimm, I lowered my head and walked faster. I didn't care about missing math anymore—I would have solved a hundred multiplication questions just to be out of the secondary school. But I was still two rows of lockers away from the handball courts and I knew she had seen me. I felt the little hairs on the back of my neck start to stand up, the way Simon's hair does when he meets an animal or a person he doesn't like. I could hear Rhea Grimm's shoes getting closer to me (she was wearing big heavy black boots like Diana's). Rhea Grimm wasn't dawdling anymore. She was a secondary kid on a mission, and that mission was me.

"Hey."

Rhea Grimm's voice snagged me from behind like it was a hook and I was a fish. I stopped and looked up. She was standing right in front of me, so close that if my hands weren't full of lunch-order tub I could have touched her. She was actually kind of pretty for someone who was so mean. She had big brown eyes, a nice nose, and her hair was long and flat and shiny. But she was wearing so much makeup that her face looked like it was covered in cake mix and paint. I wondered if that was why she was going to Mr. Bennett's office. Makeup is not part of the school uniform. Neither is jewelry and she had a lot of that, too. Thin silver bangles that clinked against each other when she moved her wrists, and three earrings in each ear.

"I know you," she said.

When she opened her mouth to speak I could see she was chewing gum. I started to tell her—in a wanting-more-than-anything-to-be-doing-multiplication voice—that I was just picking up the lunch orders and didn't want any trouble and would be on my way and thank you very much for your time. But she spoke first.

"You're Mr. Andersen's kid."

I nodded.

Rhea Grimm smiled, but not in a nice way.

"That's too bad," she said. "I mean, it must really suck. To have a dad like that."

"Like what?" I said, and even though I was trying to be brave my voice still came out like a squeak.

"You know," she said, and she leaned down so her cake-mix face was right up close to mine. "Like—*crazy.*"

Usually I'm good with words. I talk a lot and I know how to make conversation. But after Rhea Grimm said *crazy* it was like all the words I had ever known disappeared from my brain. I opened my mouth but nothing came out. And I gripped the lunch orders tightly and ran.

I ran so fast that when I got back to the classroom there was still twenty minutes of math left. I couldn't stop thinking about Rhea Grimm and I got every question wrong, and when I showed my work, it all looked like overcooked spaghetti because my hand was shaking. I didn't remember the Caramello Koala until after lunch, and when I pulled it out of my pocket its face had melted into a lopsided chocolate blob. I still ate it, but without a nose and a smiling mouth it just tasted like Caramello.

TWELVE

BECAUSE OF RHEA GRIMM, FOR THE REST of the afternoon I thought about my dad. I thought about his jokes, and the way he wears glasses when he reads our school reports, and about how he doesn't like shopping for new clothes. But mostly I thought about how I'm like him.

My dad and I are the same in a lot of good ways, like writing stories and listening to the Rolling Stones and eating strawberry ice cream out of the tub. We are also the same in some so-so ways, like having curly hair and being tall and skinny. And we are the same in one bad way, and that bad way is that we both have Those Days.

On Those Days things that I normally love doing— like having pancakes for breakfast or reading or looking for the peacocks—aren't fun anymore. Everything feels like math class: boring and complicated. On Those Days I don't want anything, which is not right, because people always want something. Mum wants to cook, and Diana wants to be on her phone, and Grandpa wants to do crosswords, and Jonas wants to go on the internet. Even animals want things—Simon wants to sniff, and birds want to fly, and worms want to wriggle. But on Those Days the only thing I want is sleep, and I only want that so I don't have to think about not-wanting anything else.

If I go to school on one of Those Days I'm not good at anything, not even reading and writing. Sometimes I can't even open my book. A lot of the teachers get angry at me but some, like Miss Shilling, just pat me on the shoulder and leave me alone. On Those Days nothing is interesting at all. If Jonas tells me a fact on one of Those Days I don't care. And usually I like to think of nice ways to describe people. For example, on a normal day if I was trying to describe Miss Shilling I might say she looks like a Christmas tree in autumn, because she is decorated in red and orange and yellow and brown. But on one of Those Days I would probably just say that Miss Shilling has a lot of necklaces.

Dad and I never talk about having Those Days the way we talk about Huck Finn or whether "Wild Horses" is a better song than "Love in Vain." But I know Dad has

Those Days, too. I know when he doesn't eat, and I know when he hasn't shaved, and I know when he doesn't read but just sits and stares at the TV and is very quiet. I want to tell him that I know about Those Days. I want to say something that will help him smile, and talk, and want things again. But I don't know what to say. And then I feel like maybe I'm not that good at words after all. And that makes me scared, because when I was little I thought words could fix everything. But now that I'm eleven-turning-twelve I'm not so sure.

After school I went looking for the peacocks with Jonas, but I couldn't concentrate. Partly because Jonas kept telling me interesting facts, but mostly because I was thinking about Rhea Grimm. So when William Shakespeare slunk out from behind a bush I didn't see him in time, and he got away.

When I got home I wanted my brain to stop thinking so I went to my room to read for a while. When I want to stop thinking, my favorite kinds of books to read are mysteries, like Sherlock Holmes and Nancy Drew. Dad doesn't like mysteries. He says they are lollipops for your brain and that I should read harder books with Themes in them, like *Lord of the Flies*. But I think that sometimes it is good to read mysteries because it gives your brain a rest from thinking about things like freedom and society and meaning. Which is important, because if you spend too much time thinking about meaning you start to get quiet and sad and you don't want to play tennis-on-a-string with your kids anymore.

At that moment I was reading a book called *The Hound of the Baskervilles*, which is a Sherlock Holmes mystery about a huge dog that goes around at night on a moor and frightens and hurts and even kills people. It's a really good story and after I had been reading it for a little while my brain stopped thinking about Rhea Grimm and started thinking about detective work and creepy old houses and Dr. Watson. I was up to the part where Dr. Watson goes to stay at the house on the moor and writes letters to Sherlock Holmes about all the things he notices. And it made me think about my own peacock mystery and about how writing things down can help when you are stuck. So I got out my Notebook for Noticing and started to write a To-Do List.

To-Do Lists are important because they help you remember things. Mum has lots of To-Do Lists but they are not about investigating. Most of her To-Do Lists she sticks on the fridge and those are lists of things like "buy carrots" or "get the fan in the bathroom fixed." She's got other To-Do Lists that she keeps in a book in a drawer next to her side of the bed. She doesn't show those To-Do Lists to anyone. Not even Dad.

My To-Do List looked like this:

1. Fill Jonas in on the things I already know about the peacocks.
2. Check out places on The Other Side of Town where Virginia and William Shakespeare might be hiding.
3. Interview people who might know important details about the peacocks.
4. Do math homework. (This wasn't part of my investigation but it was still something I had to do.)
5. Find out what Buddhism is. (This was also not part of finding the peacocks, but it was part of me trying to understand fourteen-turning-fifteen Diana. I decided to make it a Long-Term Goal, like when Mum writes in her book that she wants to "learn Spanish" or "take a break.")

After I had finished writing my To-Do List I looked at it and tried to decide what I should do first. I couldn't talk to Jonas until school tomorrow, and I couldn't check out The Other Side of Town (where I had last seen Virginia) because it was too close to dinnertime. I couldn't do my math homework because I didn't want to, and finding out about Buddhism was a Long-Term Goal that needed the internet, which I'm not allowed to have until I'm thirteen.

So the only thing on my To-Do List that I could actually do was interview people. I drew a circle around number 3 and closed my notebook.

Mum was in the kitchen doing her homework. In January Mum started taking night classes at TAFE to learn more about cooking, and her assignments were always chopping or baking or frying something. Today she was poking into a pot of pasta with a fork. The counter was covered in recipe books and notepaper and splotches of what looked like yogurt. Everything smelled like spaghetti and meatballs, only sort of bittersweet. Before she started night classes Mum's cooking was always delicious, but it was not so complicated.

"Mum?" I said.

"Yep." She was looking at the pot of pasta like it was a bomb about to explode.

"Can I interview you?"

"Just a second," she said, and then she counted under her breath "three, two, one" and lifted the pot off the stove.

"That was three seconds," I said, while she was draining the boiling water into the sink.

"What?"

"Can I interview you about the peacocks?"

"All right, I suppose so." She handed me something

that looked like a cross between an orange and a turnip. "Can you peel that?"

I stuck my thumbnail under the pointy end. "How long have you been friends with Mrs. Hudson?"

Mum got the blender out of the cupboard. "Polly? Gosh, I don't know. Since we moved here. Six, seven years."

I pulled the weirdly smooth skin of the thing Mum had given me all the way down. "And how long—" The inside of the orange-turnip was full of little pale pink pebbly things. "What is this?"

"A pomegranate," Mum said. "Here, pass me some of those seeds."

I gave her a handful of the pebbles and she put them in the blender. "How long have Mr. and Mrs. Hudson had the peacocks?"

"Quite a while," Mum said. "Five years or so." Then she pressed start on the blender, so I had to pause the interview.

While the interview was on pause I looked carefully at my mum. My mum is not tall, but not short. She is not fat, but not skinny, either. She has tanned skin and freckles all the way from the tops of her arms to her shoulders. She has really dark brown hair that she keeps cut just long enough so she can tuck the ends behind her ears. I've seen photos from when Mum was at university and her hair was so long it went all the way down to her butt. When I asked her once why she doesn't have long hair anymore she just laughed and said she's too old. My mum is thirty-nine. If you're standing far away from her you can't really tell, but up close you can see lines around her eyes and her mouth.

I never really think about my mum being beautiful. I think this is because I see her every day, and I have seen her every day since I was born. Usually when I look at her I don't see her hair and her skin and her eyes, and I don't remember that she has a Master's in History and does other things like working in the public library and writing letters to her mum and dad who live in Perth (which is so far away it is in a different time zone). I just see my mum, who is the person who buys me clothes and packs my lunch and gets annoyed at me when I am being a nuisance. Maybe if I went away for a while and then came back I would notice how beautiful she is. I know a lot of people think my mum is beautiful. Like my dad. I can tell by the way he looks at her sometimes when he thinks nobody else is watching. He gets this sort of half-smile and his eyes go faraway, the way Simon's do when he is staring at someone cooking chops on the barbecue. When Dad looks at Mum it seems like he is remembering something really, really lovely.

Mum stopped the blender and held out her hand. I

passed her some more pomegranate pebbles. "Are you and Mrs. Hudson best friends?"

"We're good friends," Mum said. She put the pomegranate pebbles in the blender.

"So you talk a lot?" I asked this question quickly, before Mum could turn the blender on again. I knew Mum and Mrs. Hudson talked a lot because Mrs. Hudson is always coming over for a cuppa, and I thought she might have told Mum a secret about the peacocks that she hadn't told me. But I didn't want Mum to know I knew, because then she might get suspicious and not tell me anything.

"I suppose so." Mum's finger was hovering over the ON switch.

"Do you tell each other everything?"

"We tell each other a lot of things."

"Secrets?"

"Now and then."

"Secrets you don't tell to anyone else? Not even me?"

"Cassandra, what does this have to do with—"

"Not even Dad?"

Mum moved her hand away from the ON switch. For a moment it seemed like she didn't know where to put it. Then she put both her hands on her hips.

"All right, that's enough. I'm busy, and you've got math homework to do."

"But I was just—"

"Off you go."

Mum pressed ON before I could say anything else. She stared at the churning pomegranate pebbles and for a minute her cheeks were the same color as the pink mush. I knew the interview was over. I put the unpeeled part of the pomegranate on the counter. For the third time since my peacock investigation began, I felt like I was close to knowing something. But I still seemed to know nothing at all.

THIRTEEN

WRITERS ARE SUPPOSED TO HELP YOU UNDERSTAND things. For example, cookbook writers help you understand how to make lemon cake and lasagna, wildlife writers help you understand why cockatoos can fly but emus can't, and space writers help you understand that the universe is bigger than anything you could ever imagine. Story writers, like me, are supposed to help you understand the characters in a story, and why they do the things they do. This is one of the hardest parts of being a writer. Especially when you *think* you know someone, but then they act in a way that is totally surprising and strange and confusing and you wonder if you ever really knew them at all.

On Friday it was Grandpa's birthday so we went to

The Very Nice Restaurant for dinner. The Very Nice Restaurant is Very Nice because you have to walk up steps to get to it (so it is a little bit higher than all the other restaurants and shops on the street) and it has its own yard with perfectly short grass and white rosebushes, although they are mostly thorns. It also has white tablecloths and a coatroom, and it doesn't have a kids' menu. The Very Nice Restaurant is actually Mum's favorite restaurant. Grandpa's favorite restaurant is staying home and watching cricket and eating fish-and-chips. But even though it was Grandpa's birthday (and even though he is Dad's dad, not Mum's), Mum still got to choose because she is the person in our family who is in charge of Special Occasions.

When we got to The Very Nice Restaurant, Roger opened the door for us. Roger is the head waiter. He has black hair that always looks wet and red hands from carrying hot plates and washing dishes. Mum knows Roger from her night classes. Sometimes he gives her a lift home and sometimes she gives him things in Tupperware containers, like peanut butter brownies or leftover roast dinner. "He's all on his own," Mum says. "It's hard cooking for one."

"Have you tried the coconut friands yet?" Roger said to Mum while he was taking our coats.

"Yes, amazing!" Mum said. "Have you tackled the jus?"

"Not yet," Roger said. "I'm waiting for some tips from the master."

"Oh. Well," Mum said (which is what she always says when she is embarrassed and doesn't know what to say).

Roger showed us to our table, and when we sat down he unfolded our white cloth napkins and put them on our laps for us. Then he went away so we could think about the wine list. A lot of people must have been celebrating Special Occasions today, because The Very Nice Restaurant was busy and noisy, which wasn't good for Grandpa because he can't hear very well in busy and noisy places. When Dad asked, "What would you like to drink, Dad?" Grandpa yelled back, "Very nice, thank you, Mark," and the Special Occasion wasn't off to a good start.

We were still waiting for our food when Grandpa almost-yelled at Diana for not going to church on Sunday. He couldn't all-the-way-yell at her for two reasons. First, we were in The Very Nice Restaurant, where even old people have to be on their best behavior. And second, Grandpa had a bad cough that kept interrupting his sentences. Every time Grandpa coughed Dad looked at Mum, and Mum looked at Diana, and Diana looked at the tablecloth. No one looked at me, which I thought was pretty rude. I felt bad for Diana, though. Grandpa is hardly ever angry with anyone, and if he is he never yells (or even almost-yells) at them.

"What are you going to do without church?" Grandpa cleared his throat. "You've got to believe in something."

"I do," Diana said in a calm, clear voice that didn't shake at all. "I believe in Buddhism."

Grandpa's lips let out a sound that was a bit like a fart and a bit like a car breaking down. "Buddhism! What sort of thing is that to believe in?"

"It's about thinking," I said, because nobody else was saying anything. (Mum was talking to Roger about the best way to stir soup and Dad was staring deep into his glass of wine like he was expecting to see something swimming in there.) But Grandpa didn't hear me.

"It's just as good as believing in church," Diana said quietly.

"No, it bloody well isn't!" This was very unlike Grandpa, because usually he swears even less than he yells. He coughed and Diana passed him a glass of water. Dad looked at Mum. Mum looked at Diana. Diana looked at the tablecloth.

"I don't want to fight with you, Grandpa," Diana said. This was really surprising because Diana (*especially* fourteen-turning-fifteen Diana) will fight with anyone if she thinks she's right. Even adults. I couldn't tell if it was the Buddhism, or The Very Nice Restaurant, or something else altogether, but Diana and Grandpa were definitely acting weird.

Then our food came and for the rest of Grandpa's birthday everyone talked about boring things like where Dad bought his shirts and how Mum could never find any fresh lemongrass in the supermarket. And the only other interesting thing that happened was that when it was time to pay, Dad whispered something to Grandpa and Grandpa gave his credit card to Roger. This was interesting because usually Mum is very strict about the person whose Special Occasion it is not paying.

Every time I looked at Grandpa after his almost-fight with Diana I got a heavy feeling in my stomach, like I had swallowed one of the shot puts we use on athletics days at school. I thought that Grandpa almost-yelling at Diana about Buddhism was not fair, since he didn't really know what Buddhism was. And usually my grandpa is really fair. My grandpa is the kind of person who helps people with their gardens and gives money to soup kitchens and lets me pass him tools when he is fixing the car. And I'm worried that when you read this chapter you will think my grandpa is not a nice character because he almost-yelled at Diana. What you don't know is that he is the kind of person you could love so much that you feel like you might burst. And that will mean you might think I'm not good at writing stories, because I haven't given you all the information you need to understand.

FOURTEEN

WRITING A STORY IS SOMETIMES LIKE BEING a detective because you have to collect a lot of information. Some of the pieces of information will turn out to be clues, and some of them will turn out to be Red Herrings. A Red Herring is something that seems important but actually isn't. It is also a kind of fish. At the start of your investigation it's hard to tell which things are clues and which are fish so you have to collect everything. But later, when you have done a lot of detecting and you start to see which direction your investigation is going in, it's easier to tell the clues from the Red Herrings. Then you can throw away the fish and solve the mystery.

It's the same when you are writing a story. At first, it

is hard to decide which details are important and which ones are superfluous (i.e. ones you don't need to understand the story). This is because sometimes you don't know what your story is about until it is finished. So you have to write down everything and when you get to the end you can go back and cross out the superfluous details.

For example, something happened the day after Grandpa's birthday dinner that felt important, even though it had nothing to do with finding Virginia and William Shakespeare. It was Saturday, and it rained. I was getting ready to meet Jonas so we could go and look for the peacocks, but when Mum saw me putting on my rain boots she said, "Oh no you don't, Cassandra Jane Andersen. Not in this weather."

"But the peacocks."

"The peacocks can wait, okay?"

It looks like a question when I write it down like that, but it really wasn't. Questions are part of discussions, and we weren't having a discussion.

"Take off those boots," said Mum. "You can help me make zucchini cake."

I wanted to point out that it wasn't really fair for me to help Mum with her homework when she hadn't helped me with mine, but I knew that would be pushing it so I went and got the flour out of the pantry instead.

Making zucchini cake wasn't as bad as I thought it

would be. Mum let me beat the egg whites into stiff peaks (which is my favorite cooking job to do) and for a little while it felt like I had gone back to last year, before Mum was always cross with me. Back then, when I helped Mum cook or plant roses or do jigsaws, I would ask "WH" questions and she would answer them. Here are some examples of the kinds of "WH" questions I used to ask Mum:

> **WH**y do people kill seals? *(Answer: for their fur and their meat.)*
> **HoW** old do you have to be to drink coffee? *(Answer: at least fifteen.)*
> **WH**at is a dust bunny? *(Answer: a ball of dust.)*
> **WH**ere is Machu Picchu? *(Answer: in Peru.)*
> **WH**en did humans land on the moon? *(Answer: 1969.)*
> **WH**o invented lightbulbs? *(Answer: Thomas Edison.)*

While I was beating egg whites on this morning I decided to ask Mum some WH questions. I was thinking about how Jonas doesn't like The Creation Story from church, but I do. So I asked Mum WHat she thought about it.

"I like it," Mum said.

"But it's not true," I said.

"Just because a story's not true doesn't mean it's not

good," Mum said. She was grating zucchini and her fingertips were green.

"Jonas says the real story is there was a Big Bang in space, and then the Earth was made out of bits of exploded rock."

"Well, that is true, scientifically," Mum said. She stopped grating and looked out the window, where Dad's car was pulling into the driveway. "The Creation Story is true in a different way. It's a Metaphor."

I started to ask WHat a Metaphor was but when I saw the way Mum was staring at Dad I stopped. I followed her eyes out the window and saw Dad shut the trunk of the car. Then the front door opened, and we could hear Dad doing something in the laundry. Mum sighed. Then Dad came into the kitchen and Mum started grating zucchini again.

"Hey, Dad," I said. "We're making zucchini cake."

Dad made a throat-clearing sound and rubbed a hand over the bits of almost-beard on his chin. He looked at Mum.

"Yum," he said, except the way he said it made it sound like he really meant "Gross."

Mum didn't look at him.

"I'll leave you to it," Dad said, and then he went into his study.

Mum stopped grating and stared at the pile of green

mush she had made on the chopping board.

"This is too much zucchini," she said, and scraped some of it into the compost bin.

And the reason this felt important was that, later, when the zucchini cake was in the oven and Mum had gone across the road to visit Mrs. Hudson, I went to the laundry and opened the cupboard to see what Dad had put in there. At first the mop and the big umbrella fell on top of me, which was normal. But then I looked up. And that was how I saw the boxes. The top shelf was full of them. They were all made of brown cardboard, and they were big, small, and medium-size. I couldn't reach any, but just seeing them sitting there gave me that heavy shot-put feeling in my stomach again. It was an out-of-place feeling. And it seemed important because we've never had so many boxes of so many sizes in our laundry cupboard before.

After I found the boxes in the cupboard, I waited in the kitchen until the timer buzzed, like Mum had asked me to, and then I turned off the oven. By then it was the afternoon and the rain had turned into a downpour. I had finished all my homework and *The Hound of the Basker-villes.* Mum was still at Mrs. Hudson's. Dad was in his study with the door shut. Diana was in her room with the door shut. And Simon was trying to hide in the kitchen cupboard because he is very scared of heavy rain, even without thunder. (Simon is allowed to be an inside dog during downpours and thunderstorms, because he is so afraid of them and might run away.) By two o'clock I was officially bored.

"Stop being such a baby," I said to Simon. Then I left him in the kitchen—half in and half out of the cupboard with his butt shaking—and went to see if I could overhear Diana talking to her not-boyfriend, aka Tom Golding.

I listened at Diana's door very quietly for a few minutes, but there was no sound coming from her room at all. I knocked (which is something Diana says I have to do because now that she is fourteen-turning-fifteen she needs privacy) but there was no answer. So—partly in case Diana was unconscious or dead but mostly because I was bored—I opened the door.

Diana was sitting in the middle of the carpet with her legs crossed. She had her arms balanced on her thighs and her palms were flat and open, the way you're supposed to have them if you're feeding sugar cubes to a horse. Her eyes were closed and she was breathing really slowly and heavily. When I saw her like that my cheeks got hot and I felt the same way I had when I walked in on Mrs. Hudson on the toilet. I wanted Diana to know I was there so it would stop being weird, so I said, "Diana." But she didn't move, so I said, "Diana!" really loud, as if I was inside and she was in the backyard. And her eyes popped open.

First Diana looked really calm. Then she looked

confused. And finally she looked angry.

"What are you doing?" she said.

"What are *you* doing?" I said back, because sometimes the best way to avoid getting into trouble is to answer a question with a question.

"I told you to knock," Diana said.

"I did!" I said. "You didn't hear me because you were . . . doing that." I pointed to the space on the carpet where Diana wasn't sitting anymore because she was standing up and trying to get me to leave.

"Well, knock louder next time." Diana pushed me toward the doorway.

"Wait!" I said. "Just tell me what you were doing. Please. I promise I'll leave you alone for the rest of the weekend if you tell me."

Diana sighed.

"Pretty please," I said. This is something Diana and I always used to say to each other before she was fourteen-turning-fifteen. "Pretty please with sprinkles and nuts and chocolate topping and wafers and sherbet and—"

Diana took a very, very deep breath and closed her eyes for a moment. "All right, fine," she said. She opened her eyes. "I was Meditating."

"What's Meditating?"

I thought Diana was going to tell me I wouldn't understand because I was only eleven-turning-twelve, but instead she said, "It's breathing and not-thinking. It's Buddhist."

I understand a lot of things, like past participles and sarcasm and the Dewey Decimal System. But one thing I definitely don't understand is not-thinking. I am always thinking. I'm thinking when I read and when I write. I'm thinking when I walk home from school, and when I'm talking to Jonas, and when I'm doing high-jump in PE. Even when I'm asleep I dream, which is basically the same as thinking except you don't get to choose what your thoughts are about. I was pretty sure that most people were like me and that they were thinking all the time, too. Was there a way to turn off your brain that I didn't know about? Like the way Diana could roll her tongue but I couldn't? Could I learn how to do it and be like Simon when he sniffed in the bush? Up until now I always thought that thinking for your brain was like beating for your heart: if it wasn't happening it was because you were dead.

I also didn't understand because Jonas had told me that Buddhism was about thinking, which meant that either Jonas was wrong, or Diana was. Which didn't make sense because Jonas and Diana are two of the smartest people I know.

I didn't say any of this to Diana because I didn't want her to think I was stupid. Instead I just nodded and went

"Hmmm" like I was thinking deeply about my opinion (the way Mrs. Atkinson does on Monday mornings when Jonas tells her all the interesting facts he has learned on the weekend). It must have worked because after a little while Diana said something else:

"It's from Aunt Sally's book."

And then something else:

"It's about Nirvana."

And finally:

"It's a place where you don't need anything."

I had never heard of a place called Nirvana before, and I know a lot about a lot of places.

"Is that in Scandinavia?" I asked, because Scandinavia is one of the places I don't know a lot about. Diana rolled her eyes.

"It's nowhere," she said. "It's in your head."

This reminded me of The Creation Story, and how Miss Robinson had explained it using a piece of black paper.

"Is it a symbol?" I asked.

"No," Diana said. "And it's not a Metaphor, either. It's a way of being."

"How can you be and not need anything?" I asked. Diana sighed and I could tell that she was losing patience with me.

"You just close your eyes and breathe and try not to

think," she said and started to nudge me out the door. "Okay? Now leave me alone for the rest of the weekend."

I walked into the kitchen and Diana shut herself back in her room. I listened to the rain and stared at Simon's shivering butt. The whole time my brain was wondering and wandering and trying-to-figure-out. After a while it figured out two things:

1. Fourteen-turning-fifteen Diana is complicated, and

2. Understanding Buddhism was going to be a much Longer Term Goal than I had thought.

FIFTEEN

IT RAINED FOR THE REST OF THE weekend, so I wrote down all the things that had happened on Saturday and started reading *To Kill a Mockingbird*. (Dad is teaching it for Year Nine English and he let me borrow his copy.) Then on Monday two things happened that made me think my luck was changing:

1. The sun came out, and
2. It was A Pupil-Free Day.

A Pupil-Free Day means kids don't go to school but teachers do so they can get work done without being distracted, work like writing reports or putting up displays or having staff meetings. So on Monday morning Dad ate his breakfast and got his bag and his keys and went to school, and Diana stayed in her room Meditating, and Mum went to the library, and Simon and I went looking for the peacocks.

I packed my backpack with water and zucchini cake. I was going to call Jonas but then I remembered that he was leaving this morning for his big overseas holiday with Peter and Irene, so I didn't. I showed Simon William Shakespeare's feather and let him sniff it. I was hoping doing this would help him find the peacocks the way letting police dogs sniff evidence helps them find criminals. But Simon just looked confused, and when I pushed the feather closer to his nose he sneezed all over it. Simon is definitely not police-dog material.

While we were walking, Simon had his nose down deep in the leaves. He moved really fast and sniffed a lot, and he kind of looked and sounded like a vacuum cleaner. I liked the idea that we were vacuuming for clues. We vacuumed all the way along the river in one direction and all the way back again in the other. We vacuumed off the track and into the bush and under logs and into wombat holes. We vacuumed for so long that the sun climbed right up into the middle of the sky and my stomach started grumbling. We hadn't found any clues, and I was about to suggest that it was time for zucchini cake. But then Simon stopped and stood very still.

Simon never stops and stands still, unless something

important is happening, like Dad opening a can of dog food or Aunt Sally's car pulling into our driveway. The only thing that moved was Simon's pink nose—it twitched, and its nostrils got wider, and the little hairs on the end of it stood up and reached forward like they were arrows pointing toward a smell. My eyes followed Simon's nose across the river and between two gum trees. And standing there, with his tail folded up and his wings tucked against him, was William Shakespeare.

It took the rest of Simon a while to catch up with his nose (because Simon is a Brittany spaniel, smell is his best sense), but when it did he started running, and there was nothing I could do except hold on to his lead and run too. After smelling, Simon's best skill is being strong, so when he started pulling us down the bank toward William Shakespeare I knew I had no hope. I was going in the river.

It wasn't as cold as I expected it to be, but it was as wet. I landed on my butt and yelled "Ow!" and that was when Simon finally stopped and turned around to look at me. His face was a mix of "What are you doing in the river?" and "Hurry up!"

I quickly checked to make sure there were no crayfish nearby and then hauled myself out of the water. Across the river William Shakespeare was still standing between the gum trees. He was looking at us with his head on one side like he was trying to figure out what we were doing. Then Simon barked and William Shakespeare let out a loud *Liiieeaaaaaawww!* sound and ran off into the bush.

By the time we got out of the water and up the bank and through the trees William Shakespeare was nowhere to be seen. Simon looked at me with the same face he has when he thinks he's getting a bone and it turns out to be a worm tablet.

William Shakespeare had led us to The Other Side of Town. We vacuumed slower (because we were disappointed and because I was waterlogged) past the bank, and The Very Nice Restaurant, and Lee Street, and the bus station. When we got to the hospital we sat down for a rest. Simon licked my wet shoes and I gave him some zucchini cake. Then I tried to decide what to do next.

While we were sitting and eating and thinking, a car door slammed. I looked up. Across the road was a red station wagon, which is exactly the kind of car that my dad drives. And walking away from the red station wagon—even though he should have been photocopying or cleaning his desk or having a meeting at school—was my dad.

When Simon saw Dad he started whimpering and pulling on the lead and trying to get to him. But something about the look on Dad's face and the direction he was walking in made me think he wouldn't be happy to see us. And the direction he was walking in was past the hospital and up the little path and through the little gate and into The Clinic.

I pulled Simon behind some bushes and knelt down. We watched Dad walk—in his brown going-to-work shoes with his brown going-to-work bag. And he looked exactly like my dad in every way except that he was in a place I'd never seen my dad go, making a face I'd never seen my dad make. We watched until the door of The Clinic closed behind him, and until the shot put in my stomach was so heavy I thought I might throw up.

The only thing I could think to do next was go home. So I packed up the zucchini cake and the water and William Shakespeare's feather.

And we went.

SIXTEEN

SOMETIMES THOSE DAYS HAPPEN FOR NO REASON, but sometimes something makes them happen. For example, seeing
your dad do something you have never seen your dad do
before. Something so strange that it is disturbing (which
is the name of the feeling you get when you see a cat play
with a moth for twenty minutes before pulling its wings
off and then not even eating it). So strange that you have
to go home straightaway and get into bed and stare at the
ceiling and try to understand what it means.

When I woke up this morning I still didn't understand,
and I still didn't want to get out of bed. And that was
when I knew Tuesday was one of Those Days.

When Mum came in to find out why I wasn't in the

shower yet I lied and told her that I had thrown up so she wouldn't make me go to school. She put her hand on my head and then she made me some toast with Vegemite (no butter) and some flat lemonade. I wasn't going to tell Mum that I couldn't go to school because I didn't feel like it. If you say that to mums they just say: "Too bad, everyone does things they don't want to do sometimes." But there is a difference between not wanting to do some things and Those Days. On a normal day I don't want to do things like eat Brussels sprouts or do math or walk to school, but then I do them and it's not really that bad, just kind of annoying. But when you have to do things on one of Those Days, even things you normally love, it really, really hurts. But it doesn't hurt in a place you can show to your mum or a doctor, like Diana's arm did when she broke it two years ago falling off the monkey bars. It just hurts everywhere inside you and makes you want to cry, but you don't because you can't point to the pain and no one can help you.

This morning while I was lying on my bed I tried breathing and not-thinking, but my brain kept going back to Monday afternoon. First it thought about chasing William Shakespeare and falling in the river, which was easy. Then it thought about having a rest and eating zucchini cake with Simon, which was pretty easy, too. Then it thought about seeing Dad get out of the car, which was a bit harder. And finally it thought about seeing Dad go into The Clinic, which was very hard. I closed my eyes really tight to try and help my brain understand, but all I could think about was the car door slamming and Dad walking when he was supposed to be marking essays. My brain was stuck. It felt like writing a story and not being able to figure out the ending.

By the time it was afternoon I was sick of being stuck and I was also thirsty, so I went to the kitchen for a glass of water. Mum was having a cup of tea with Mrs. Hudson.

"I don't know how else to explain it," Mum said while I was stopped in the hallway. "It's like something's frozen, inside me, and no matter what I do I can't get it to thaw out again."

"These things happen," Mrs. Hudson said. "Especially given the circumstances."

"He won't talk about it. He hardly talks to me at all anymore. I just don't know what else to do."

"It's okay." Mrs. Hudson put her hand on my mum's. "You can't blame yourself."

"I'm worried about the girls," Mum said. "Cassie, in particular. I don't think she'll understand."

"She understands a lot more than you think," said Mrs. Hudson (who I always knew was not just nice but also smart). "She'll be all right."

"Be honest," Mum said. "Do you think I'm being selfish?"

"Not at all," said Mrs. Hudson.

Mum sighed. "I just need to do something different," she said. "I think it'll be best for everyone."

Mrs. Hudson noticed me standing in the doorway. "Hello there, Peacock Detective," she said. "How's the investigation going?"

I tried to sound positive, even though I wasn't feeling it. "I almost caught William Shakespeare," I said. "But then Simon pulled me into the river."

Mrs. Hudson smiled. "Never mind," she said. "You can't rush peacocks."

Mum was looking at me, but her eyes weren't meeting mine. "Are you feeling any better?" she asked.

"Yes," I said, and then I turned around and walked back down the hallway to my room. I had forgotten all about my glass of water. I was thinking about what Mum had said earlier: *I just need to do something different.*

Dad told me once that when you are writing and you get stuck the best thing to do is to think about your story in a different way. For example, last year for school I was writing a story about jungle explorers. I had written the beginning and the middle and I was getting close to the end where the jungle explorers were about to be eaten by a tiger. I didn't want them to be eaten, but I had written them into the situation and I didn't know how to get them out of it. So I thought about the story in a different way. The most different thing that I could think of from a jungle explorer was a city dweller (which is a fancy way of saying someone who lives in a city). And then I remembered that at the start of the story the jungle explorers had met some tourists from the city, and the jungle explorers didn't like the tourists because they were noisy and messy and were driving through the jungle in a big bus. And then I had an idea that the tourists would come back into the story in their big bus and scare away the tiger and save the jungle explorers. So I stopped being stuck and the jungle explorers didn't get eaten and it was all because I thought in a different way.

Back in my room I sat down and closed my eyes and thought about Dad again, but differently. I thought about the red station wagon, and the parking lot, and The Clinic. I thought about his clothes, and his face, and his walk. I thought about all the times he locked himself in his study, and how he was always staying up late, and I thought about the cardboard boxes in the laundry cupboard. After I had thought differently for a long time I started to get an idea. And as my idea grew all the little details stuck together and made sense, and I got the same kind of warm, glowing feeling that comes from writing a really good story.

By teatime I wasn't having one of Those Days anymore. I understood what seeing Dad getting out of the red station wagon and going into The Clinic meant. And what it meant was this:

My dad is a spy.

For three weeks I didn't do much peacock detecting. Partly because the weather was getting colder but mostly because I was busy confirming my suspicions about Dad. First I wrote down details in my Notebook for Noticing:

Friday 22 March

—Dad seemed tired this morning.

Wednesday 27 March

—Dad took two sick days this week.

Thursday 4 April

—Dad didn't finish his pork cutlets.

Then I did a lot of imagining and dot-connecting to straighten everything out. I don't know about Themes in books, but I do know about spies in books, and I know that spies sometimes have to work late (which makes them tired) and at inconvenient times (like during school hours or at dinnertime). I also know that spies can't tell anyone that they are spies, not even their families. This means that they have to live double lives: one life where they are a spy and one life where they are something else (like an English literature teacher). Based on this information I was able to deduce (which means figure out) that my dad is a spy. I was also able to deduce that he is working on a very important case, which explains why he spends so much time in his study, and why I had seen him in a place he shouldn't have been in, and why he is filling the laundry cupboard with cardboard boxes.

In those three weeks a few other interesting things happened. The first was that I found two more of William Shakespeare's feathers on the way to school. The second was that Jonas sent me a postcard that said *Did you know Greece is one of the biggest producers of sponges?* And the third was that the school holidays started and it was Easter.

On Easter Sunday morning we always have an egg hunt. Dad hides eggs through the house—in vases and behind the couch and on windowsills. But this morning when I woke up there were four Creme Eggs sitting on the kitchen counter.

"Two for you and two for your sister," Mum said while she was making coffee. "Happy Easter."

I picked up one of my Creme Eggs and examined it. "What about the egg hunt?"

Mum sipped her coffee. "Mark."

Dad was sitting on the couch watching TV. He cleared his throat. "We thought you might be getting a bit old for egg hunting," he said. He was talking to me but he was looking at Mum.

Mum just drank more coffee and said, "Get dressed, Cassie. We're going to be late for church."

So I went to church on Easter Sunday without Diana

and without an egg hunt. The good news was that Grandpa was there and I got to sit next to him and share his hymn-book. He didn't sing as loud as usual and he was tired so he didn't stand up for the standing-up bits. But it was nice to hear his singing voice, and he told me an Easter joke that went: "Why did the Easter egg hide? Because he was a little chicken," which I thought was funny. After church Grandpa came to our house for Easter Sunday lunch.

While we were eating sundried tomatoes and olives for entree I sat on Grandpa's good side, so he would hear me, and said, "I only got two chocolate eggs this year." I was talking to Grandpa but I was looking at Dad.

Grandpa ate an olive and then wiped his mouth with a napkin. "Some people won't get any eggs, Cassie. Did you see Mrs. Grimm at church? Her kids'll be lucky to get two eggs between them."

"Such a nice lady," Mum said while she was taking away our small plates and giving us big ones. "Mark teaches her daughter, the eldest one."

Dad was studying his place mat and probably planning his next spy mission. "Hmm?"

Mum sighed. "Angela Grimm's girl. What's her name?"

"Rhea," Dad said. "What a nightmare."

"That's understandable," Grandpa said. "Given the circumstances."

"What circumstances?" I asked.

Mum changed the subject to main course. "Who wants chicken, who wants ham?"

I turned to Diana and said, "What circumstances?"

"You wouldn't understand," Diana said. I made a face at her, but she just closed her eyes and breathed in and out and ignored me. Diana was being more annoying than usual. She didn't even seem to care that we had only got two Easter eggs each, and she even gave one of hers to Grandpa.

"Chicken or ham?" Mum was standing in front of me with a platter and a pair of tongs.

"Ham," I said, and she plonked two pieces on my plate.

"Diana?"

"No thanks," Diana said.

"No thanks, what?" Mum said.

"I don't want chicken or ham," Diana said. "I'm vegetarian."

Mum perched the tongs on the platter. "Since when?"

"Since I don't want to eat meat anymore."

Mum sighed. "Get yourself some roast veggies then," she said, and moved on to Grandpa. "Chicken or ham?"

Grandpa was about to choose chicken (because chicken is his favorite) when Dad said, "What do you mean, you're vegetarian?"

The whole Easter Sunday lunch went quiet then, because it was the longest sentence Dad had said all day.

"Your mother's been cooking for hours and you're not going to eat?" Dad's voice was getting louder, the way it does when he talks about The Liberals.

Diana's voice was quiet and still, like a pond. "Yes. Sorry, Mum."

"It's fine," Mum said.

"No, it isn't," Dad said. "You'll eat all your lunch, Diana, or you won't eat anything."

Diana pushed her chair back and stood up. She looked at Dad from her side of the table, and Dad looked at Diana from his. It was like they were having a staring contest, except it wasn't fun and no one was going to laugh when it was over. After what felt like ages Dad looked down at his big plate, and Diana left the table and went to her room.

"For God's sake—what was all that about?" Mum said.

"She's just trying to be difficult," Dad said, except the way he said it sounded like he really meant "I'm tired and I don't want to talk anymore."

Mum shook her head. "I seem to remember a time when *you* were a vegetarian."

Dad didn't say anything. He didn't eat anything, either. He just sat and stared at his plate of chicken and roast potatoes like it was a very deep, very dark hole. Mum and Grandpa and I ate the rest of our Easter Sunday lunch in silence, and later—when I was helping Mum clear the table and wash the dishes—Dad went into his study and shut the door.

SEVENTEEN

A WEEK LATER THE HOLIDAYS WERE OVER and Jonas was back.
I found him on The Snake Stairs at lunchtime eating a
cheese sandwich. When he saw me the first thing he said
was "Did you know, family holidays are *the worst*?"

This was more of an opinion than a fact, and it was an
opinion I didn't agree with since in my experience family
holidays are the best. But I didn't want to disagree with
Jonas on his first day back, so instead I stomped loudly
to scare away the snake and sat down on the other side of
the footpath and yelled, "Really?"

"Don't you have any lunch?" Jonas said.

I did, but I didn't want to eat it. Mum had packed me
the leftovers from her cooking homework, and it was a
big mess of things I didn't know the names of and didn't

like the taste of. There was some kind of casserole, and bits of chicken wrapped in leaves, and some soup. The soup would have been okay if it hadn't been purple. Mum used to pack me egg salad sandwiches and fruit, which wasn't fancy, but at least I liked it.

"I ate already," I said. I think Jonas knew I was lying, because he threw me some of his sandwich and half his banana.

While I ate I listened to Jonas complain about his family holiday. Because Jonas doesn't have any brothers or sisters his parents can afford to take him on big, overseas holidays. I'm not going to tell you exactly what he said, because a lot of it was repetitive and a lot more of it wasn't very nice. Instead, I'm going to summarize, which means just giving the most important points. And the most important points from Jonas's family holiday were:

1. France is boring.
2. Germany is boring.
3. Italy is boring.
4. Greece is boring, and
5. Peter and Irene are boring, stupid, and lame. (I don't know Jonas's parents very well, but they are always really nice to me. Plus, they bought Jonas his own computer and Wi-Fi, and they let him watch whatever he wants. But they are not my parents, so I don't get to decide if

they are boring and stupid and lame or not.)

After Jonas stopped complaining I filled him in on everything that had happened while he was away, like Buddhism being about not needing anything, and Diana Meditating and becoming a vegetarian, and finding two more feathers, and not having an egg hunt on Easter Sunday, and almost catching William Shakespeare but falling in the river instead. The last thing I told Jonas about was Dad. I told Jonas about Dad being tired and busy, and about the boxes, and about seeing him at The Clinic on a Pupil-Free Day. And I told Jonas that I'm almost-definitely-certainly-sure my dad is a spy.

While I was talking Jonas didn't say anything. He just stared into the bushes at the bottom of the steps, like he was looking for the tiger snake. I knew he was listening, though, because he had the same expression on his face that he has in science, which is his favorite subject. When I was finished Jonas didn't say anything for a long time. In that long time I started to get scared that he was going to tell me I was lying and get up and go away and not be my friend anymore.

But then he said, "Let's do a stakeout."

My stomach squirmed. Suddenly the banana and the cheese sandwich weren't getting along so well. "A stakeout?"

"Yeah, like detectives do when they want to find out

more information," Jonas said. "We can stake out your dad and find out if he really is a spy."

"Maybe we should stake out the peacocks instead," I said, since this story is about looking for the peacocks, and not about my dad.

"We can look for the peacocks on the way," Jonas said. "Don't you want to find out The Truth?"

I wasn't sure if I did. On one hand, thinking about going back to The Other Side of Town and staking out my dad gave me the heavy shot-put feeling in my stomach. But on the other hand, I really wanted to be friends with Jonas, and going on a stakeout with him would mean doing more stuff outside of school together, which would make us real friends instead of just friends because of school and because our dads know each other. It would mean Jonas was choosing to be my friend, and that felt very important.

The bell rang for the end of lunchtime. Jonas was looking at me with big eyes, the kind of eyes he gets when he learns a new shark fact. I looked down at the stairs and for a second I thought I saw the snake sliding behind them. But when I stared harder there was nothing.

"Cassie?"

I looked at Jonas. The bell was ringing in my ears, and my stomach was heavy, and Jonas was so excited. And even though I wasn't really sure I said, "Okay."

And then we went and did math for the rest of the afternoon, which is Jonas's favorite subject but not mine.

All week the only thing I could think about was the stakeout. On Wednesday Mrs. Atkinson had to tell me to turn the page twice while we were reading about ancient Greece, and when Mr. Kipling asked me in Japanese what the word for telephone was I said *kousakuin*, which is the word for spy. Every day after school Jonas and Simon and I went walking on the track by the river to look for Virginia and William Shakespeare, but Jonas was so distracted by talking about the stakeout and I was so distracted by worrying about the stakeout and Simon was so distracted by pinecones and wombat smells that by the time we noticed the peacocks they had already disappeared into the bush.

On Thursday when Mum asked me to help her beat eggs I beat them so much they went stiff and Mum had to throw them away. She didn't want me to help her anymore after that. Mum has been getting really busy with cooking. She started working less at the library so she could cook more. Some days she cooks from the time I go to school in the morning until the time I come home. The fridge is always full. And if something doesn't fit Mum takes it across the road to Mrs. Hudson, or puts it in a Tupperware container in the freezer for Roger. She writes his name on all the containers: Roger Chicken-Almond Casserole, Roger Camembert Tart, Roger Asparagus Quiche. Our freezer is full of Roger.

Dad is still Dad, except whenever I look at him my stomach feels heavy. He does the same Dad things he always does, like marking essays and watching documentaries and shaving. Most of the time now he is a serious sort of dad, but sometimes he is still a fun sort of dad, like when he made a joke about Diana's new, very short haircut. (He said she looked like a hedge that had been trimmed.) He even laughed a little bit, and I laughed a lot, and Mum and Diana didn't laugh at all.

Diana is getting closer to fifteen and further from fourteen every day. She said she cut her hair short because she didn't need long hair and she didn't care what other people thought. She is Meditating more (I can tell because she is always in her room with the door shut and no music) and she is still being vegetarian, even when Mum cooks chicken schnitzel with mushroom sauce, which is Diana's favorite. When Tom Golding calls, Diana says she is too busy to talk, even though all she is doing is breathing and not-thinking. And then one night while we were eating dinner Diana made an announcement:

"I'm moving out."

I stopped chewing. Mum looked up from the cookbook she was reading. Dad dropped his fork.

"What?" Dad had his serious face on.

"I'm moving out. Of the house," Diana said.

"You're fourteen," Mum said. "Where on Earth would you go?"

"The backyard," Diana said. "I don't want to live inside anymore. I don't need all these *things*"—she said the word "things" like it was the word "snot"—"in my life."

"I see," Dad said. "So you're going to live outside. With no electricity."

"Yes."

"No TV."

"Yes."

"Where will you sleep?"

"In the tent."

"You'll freeze," said Mum.

"No, I won't," said Diana. "I've got two sleeping bags. And I'll take the extra blankets from the spare room."

"This is ridiculous." Dad picked up his fork from the floor and wiped it with his napkin. "You're not living in the backyard. Helen?"

Dad was looking at Mum, but Mum was looking at Diana. She had a half-smile on her face, the same half-smile she gets when she looks at photos of her and Dad before they were married and she had hair down to her butt and shorts up to her hair.

"Helen?" Dad repeated.

And then Mum said something that surprised everyone, even Diana.

"Why not? Sounds like an adventure."

Then she started clearing the table while the rest of us
sat there with eyes like balloons about to burst.

"Who wants dessert?" Mum said.

And that's how Diana started to live in the backyard.

EIGHTEEN

A WEEK AFTER I SAW DAD AT The Clinic, Jonas decided we should do the stakeout. He said we should do it at two o'clock, because that was the time I had seen Dad on The Pupil-Free Day. We would have to leave school early, since the bell for home time doesn't ring until three twenty-five. We synchronized our watches so that they would show exactly the same time and we wouldn't be late. At school I couldn't concentrate at all, and I got into trouble five times (two times from Mrs. Atkinson for not listening while she explained long division, and three times from Mr. Harper in music because I kept coming in late with the triangle). All morning I thought about calling off the stakeout, but then I remembered that Jonas was my friend and that he knew lots of interesting facts and had come to my birthday party dressed as the God of the Sea. So at one o'clock I breathed in and out a lot and went to meet Jonas at the gate.

When I found him he handed me a rock.

"What's this for?" I said.

"It's a Special Stone," Jonas replied. I looked more closely. It didn't seem very special—it was gray with flecks of brown, a little bumpy at one end and smooth at the other.

"It's just a river rock," I said.

"Yes, but look." Jonas held out another rock. He pushed the side of his palm against mine, so both rocks were side by side. And then I saw the special thing. The rocks were exactly the same. They both had brown flecks in the same places, and they were both bumpy and smooth at the same ends.

"I found them," Jonas said. "That one's for you. If we get separated, leave your stone as a clue. No one else will notice it, only me. Okay?"

I nodded and looked down at my Special Stone like it was a diamond. The thought that Jonas and I were the only people who knew these stones were special made me smile right to the corners of my mouth.

"What did you tell Mrs. Atkinson?" Jonas asked me while we were walking out of school and across the road.

I tucked my Special Stone into my backpack. The sky

was getting dark and the air had that prickly, before-rain feeling. "That I had to go to the dentist," I said. "What about you?"

"That Peter and Irene were taking me to volunteer at the old people's home."

"Why do you call your mum and dad Peter and Irene?" I decided, now that Jonas and I were outside-of-school-friends, that this was a question I could ask.

"They're not my mum and dad." Jonas kicked a stick so hard he almost hit a duck that had wandered away from the river.

"Why not?"

"Why do you think?"

I hadn't thought, because to me Jonas's parents were always just Jonas's parents.

"Because they're robots?" I tried. "Because they're aliens?"

"Don't be stupid," Jonas said (which hurt a bit, because Jonas had never called me stupid before). "Because I'm adopted."

We walked in silence for a little while. I knew what adopted meant because I had read *The Adventures of Huckleberry Finn*. In that book the main character Huck is adopted because his mum is dead and his dad is an alcoholic. But I had never thought about Jonas being adopted before.

"Are your real parents dead?" I asked.

"No," Jonas said.

"Are they alcoholics?"

Jonas gave me a weird sideways look and said, "No."

"Where are they, then?" If my mum had been walking with us she would have said, "That's enough, Cassandra," because I was asking a lot of questions about a sensitive subject. But she wasn't, so she couldn't.

"I don't know," Jonas said.

We were at the bridge then, and I couldn't think of any more questions to ask so we walked across the river to The Other Side of Town without talking. I was wondering about Jonas's real parents and where they were. Maybe they were in the Amazon, or maybe they were secret scientists working for the government, or maybe they were deep-sea explorers. And even though Jonas wasn't talking I was pretty sure he was wondering about the same thing I was. And that was a nice feeling.

We walked right through The Other Side of Town wondering together but not talking. I looked for the peacocks but there were no signs of them anywhere—not even a feather or a pile of poo. For some reason not-seeing Virginia and William Shakespeare made the sky seem darker and the air more prickly.

When we got to The Clinic we set up our stakeout behind the bushes across the road, which was where Simon and I had hidden on The Pupil-Free Day. Jonas had biscuits in his bag that Irene had made, and we ate some while we were waiting. (I thought they were delicious, but Jonas said they were too chocolaty.) Jonas had also brought a pen and some paper so he could write down things we noticed on our stakeout. He wrote the day and the date, and where we were. I asked him if he had ever done investigating before, since he seemed to know a lot about being a detective.

"A bit," he said. I didn't ask where or why because I thought he would tell me if he wanted to. He didn't, which made me wonder if maybe he was a spy, too.

It was getting late in the afternoon, past the time when Simon and I had seen Dad on The Pupil-Free Day. I was worried about two things that were opposites (and not the good kind). The first worry was that Dad wouldn't come, and that Jonas would think I was stupid and a liar and wouldn't want to do stuff outside of school with me again. The second worry was that Dad would come.

We waited behind the bushes for ages while the sky got darker.

"Maybe he's not coming," I said.

"Just wait," Jonas said.

"We don't have an umbrella," I said. "The biscuits will get wet. Maybe we should just—"

"Look!" Jonas pointed across the road. Dad's car was driving into the parking lot. "There." Jonas got his pen ready. "That's your dad, right?"

I nodded and swallowed hard. I watched Dad get out

of the car and walk across the parking lot in exactly the same way he had on The Pupil-Free Day.

"See?" I said. My voice was shaking a bit. "Probably important spy business. I guess we should get going."

Jonas stood up. I was hoping he would say "Let's get out of here before we get rained on," or "I've got to get home and look up some interesting facts on the internet." But he didn't say anything like that.

Instead he turned to me, with his eyes big and bright behind his glasses, and said, "Let's follow him."

Sometimes I think Jonas is really smart, like when he tells me the scientific names of whales or when he makes magnets or does magic tricks. And other times I think he is not smart at all, like when he says things like "Let's follow him" after I've already told him my dad is a spy and that spies deal with dangerous people who do dangerous things.

"We'd better not," I said. "Let's wait here for a bit. We can have another biscuit—"

But Jonas was already walking across the road. For a moment I didn't know what to do. I felt that following Dad was a bad idea, but something else was telling me that letting Jonas go by himself might be a worse one. I ran across the road and caught up with him.

He was standing out front at the little gate, which was

open. All he had to do was walk through the gate and up the path and inside, and he would see my dad.

"Jonas, wait," I said.

"What?" Jonas turned around.

"You can't go in there."

"Why not?"

I had to think for a long moment before I could answer him. "Because they're doing experiments. Dangerous experiments. Like, with radiation. And animals."

Jonas shook his head. "No, they're not."

"Really! That's what my dad's been spying on. They're trying to make super-beasts, for the army. Dogs with two heads, and horses with shark teeth. If you go in there you'll get hurt."

"No, I won't."

"The super-beasts are dangerous. They're like . . . like . . ." I tried to find a simile that would really frighten Jonas, but my thoughts were going so fast that I couldn't think of any words at all.

"Like what?" Jonas asked.

I sighed, and my breath came out shaky. "Jonas, please just don't go in there."

"Why not?" Jonas looked confused. "Don't you want to know what your dad's doing?"

I guess I'm not a very good detective after all, since good detectives are supposed to want to solve the mystery they are investigating. But I didn't want to solve this mystery. What I wanted to do was go home, and pat Simon, and sit in my room where everything was brown and quiet. I wanted to be like Diana, sitting and breathing and not-thinking.

But I couldn't say this to Jonas, so instead I said, "No."

"But why?"

"Just."

"Just" is not a full sentence. "Just" is a word that is trying to get out of explaining. It is an excuse word. Sometimes when kids in my dad's English class don't do their homework and my dad asks them why not, they say "Just." Then my dad says, "Just is not good enough," and he makes them write an essay explaining why they didn't do their homework using reasons and examples and transition words. As soon as I said "Just" to Jonas I felt my cheeks go red because I knew that it wasn't good enough. But I wasn't brave enough to do any better.

Then Jonas said something that made my fingers and toes go cold.

"Don't you want to know The Truth?"

I know a lot of things. One thing I know is that The Truth is right, and lying is wrong. But at that moment The Truth didn't feel right at all. It felt like how you swallow eight spiders every year, only you don't know because you swallow them in your sleep. And if you don't know, then you can't feel disturbed or sick. And if I went home without going through the gate and up the path and in the door I wouldn't know The Truth. But I also wouldn't feel like my stomach was full of spiders.

So even though my head was thinking all of these thoughts the only one I said to Jonas was "No."

And then I turned and walked away.

NINETEEN

ON MY WAY HOME FROM THE STAKEOUT the rain started, and it soaked me right down to the soles of my shoes. A big part of me wanted to turn back and say I was sorry and tell Jonas a story and ask him to tell me a fact. But I didn't. I imagined Jonas walking through the gate and up the path and in the door. And I wondered if I would ever be able to talk to him again, knowing that he knew The Truth, and I didn't.

After the stakeout I worked really hard not to think about Jonas, or The Clinic, or chocolate biscuits. I made myself busy by practicing all the songs in the recorder book for music, and memorizing a half-hour talk in Japanese about tea ceremonies, and making a diorama of convict settlements for my First Fleet project. I tried Meditating like Diana, but I couldn't stop my brain from thinking, so I read *Sherlock Holmes* instead. I looked for the peacocks every day but they must have been hiding on The Other Side of Town because I never saw them. At school I didn't go near The Snake Stairs, and when Mrs. Atkinson asked Jonas and me to pick up the lunch orders from the canteen I pretended I had a stomachache so I didn't have to go.

A lot of time passed like this, so much time that April ended and May began, and the peacocks were still missing. All of the leaves, except from the gum trees, changed color and fell on the ground, so now when you stepped on them they made a crunchy dead sound. The weather got properly cold, the kind of cold where there is frost on the grass in the mornings and Simon's water bucket freezes across the top and makes him bump his nose when he tries to have a drink. It is also the kind of cold that makes Grandpa's cough worse, which means he has to stay at home most of the time, which means he can't come to church or visit us for dinner.

Diana is still living in the backyard. I think Dad thought she would move back inside after one night, but she didn't. Not after two nights, either. She comes into the house to eat and to help Mum with the dishes, but that's all. On the 14th of May Diana officially turned fifteen, but she said she didn't need a party. So Mum cooked a special vegetarian dinner and we sang "Happy Birthday" with a candle in a piece of zucchini cake. Diana didn't invite any of her friends—not even Tom Golding.

When Mum isn't at night classes she takes Diana treats in Tupperware containers and they sit in the tent together wrapped in blankets and talk for a long time.

Mum stopped working at the library so she could spend more time cooking. She filled the pantry with ingredients that I have never heard of, like galangal and wasabi and liquid smoke, and she decorates our dinner plates with flowers and herbs and fruit skins.

Dad is just Dad. He goes to school, and he goes to his study. And that's all.

Even though I'm trying not to think about Jonas, I really miss him. I miss talking to him on The Snake Stairs, and walking with him to get lunch orders, and hearing him say "Did you know . . ." all the time. I think he misses me, too, because every now and then at school he looks at me and opens his mouth like he is about to tell me a fact, but then he remembers the stakeout and closes it again.

The only thing that makes me feel a little bit better about missing Jonas is thinking that us not-being-friends anymore is an example of Cause and Effect. An Effect is the thing that happens, and a Cause is why it happens.

"Because" is a Cause and Effect transition word. Jonas and I stopped being friends be*cause* of the stakeout. The *Cause* of us not being friends was the stakeout, and a Cause is a Reason, and a Reason is something I can understand.

There are some things that happen, though, that don't have a Cause. When those kinds of things happen you can't use transition words like "because" and "so" and "therefore" to help explain them. They are completely meaningless, and trying to understand them is like trying to chew cotton candy—as soon as you have it in your mouth it dissolves into sugar-saliva and slips down your throat. When people try to explain meaningless things their mouths get twisted and all their words slip away and they can't finish their sentences.

Today one of those things happened in America. A man went to eat lunch at a restaurant and after he finished his lunch he opened his bag and took out a gun and killed forty-five people. And nobody knows why he did this, or why he talked to a lady about barbecue sauce first, or why he bothered to put his knife and fork neatly together on his plate when he was just going to make a big mess straight afterward.

When they started talking about America on the news tonight Mum told me to go to my room.

"Why?" I said.

"This isn't suitable," Mum said, which is what she says about movies that are on after nine thirty and CDs that have EXPLICIT LANGUAGE stickers and some of the books Dad gives me.

"Let her watch it, Helen," Dad said. He was wearing his glasses. "All the kids'll be talking about it tomorrow, anyway."

"She's too young," Mum said. She came out from behind the counter, where she had been making hummus. "She won't understand."

"No one understands this," Dad said.

"I understand lots of things," I said. "Like triple time and Japanese and Cause and Effect."

"There are some things you can't understand until you're older," Mum said.

"But I am older," I said. "I can read and write at a Year Seven level." I saw Dad smile a little bit when I said that, but he tried not to show it to Mum.

"She's got a point," Dad said.

"She's not mature enough, Mark."

Mum was standing with one hand on the counter and the other on her hip. She was looking at Dad the way she does when he's not allowed to say no. Dad looked at me, and then at the TV, where a reporter in America was having trouble finishing her sentences.

"Your mum's right, Cassie," he said. "You'd better go to your room."

So I did, but I didn't shut the door. And from the door-way I could hear Mum and Dad talking. And what they said went like this:

Dad: I think we should tell her about Dad.

Mum: No.

Dad: It's not fair.

Mum: She's only eleven.

Dad: She's old enough.

Mum: She's still a child.

Silence except for the TV, which said, "We thought they were letting off cannons, and . . ."

Dad: I don't think there's much time left.

Silence.

The TV said, "You don't think it's ever gonna be . . . as bad as . . ."

Mum: Mark. I'm sorry.

The TV said, "Awful, just very, very . . ."

And then I shut the door.

TWENTY

THE LAST SUNDAY IN MAY, ALMOST ONE month after the meaningless thing happened in America, was the day I opened the boxes in the laundry cupboard.

It was cold and rainy, more winter than autumn. Diana was reading in her tent, Dad was in his study, and Mum was cooking something that smelled like nail polish. I had finished all my homework and read *Jane Eyre*, and the only other thing I wanted to do was look for the peacocks. So, even though I knew Mum wouldn't like me going-out-in-this-weather, I went to the laundry to get the big umbrella.

Usually when I open the laundry cupboard the mop and the umbrella fall on top of me, but today they didn't.

And they didn't because they weren't in the cupboard. And they weren't in the cupboard because there wasn't any space for them. And there wasn't any space for them because the cupboard was full—from floor to ceiling— with cardboard boxes.

I hadn't forgotten about the boxes. I remembered them whenever I walked past the laundry, which was a lot. And every time I remembered them I tried not to imagine what was in them. Most of the time this didn't work, and my brain imagined anyway. It imagined stolen money, and it imagined whiskey (which is what Huck Finn's dad was an alcoholic for), and it imagined guns. For more than two months most of me didn't want to open the boxes, and some of me (the some of me that was still a detective) did. But today when I saw how full the shelves in the laundry cupboard were and how easily I could reach them, the scales inside me shifted. Suddenly only some of me didn't want to open the boxes, and most of me did.

I closed the laundry door just in case Mum came looking for me, and then I took a box from the shelf where the spare pillowcases used to live. It was just a plain brown cardboard box, not very big, with no wrapping but with a price sticker that said $25.95. It was kind of heavy in my hands, like an unboiled egg. I got ready to open the lid. My brain was imagining illegal drugs and casino chips and dead fish. I poked my fingernail under the little cardboard latch and pulled.

Inside, lying on a scrunched-up bed of white tissue paper, was a little elephant. It was gray, and it had its trunk in the air. I picked it up, and it was hard and cold in my hand. It was a really good elephant, with lots of details like the creases in its skin and the whites in its eyes. I put it back on the tissue paper and opened another box. In it was a small pink pig with a curly tail. In the next box there was a robin sitting on a branch. In the next box was a little girl holding a balloon. In the next box there was an airplane.

I opened ten boxes altogether. Inside all of them were ornaments, the kind you put on window ledges and mantelpieces to brighten-up-your-home. Some of them were cheap, but some of them were very expensive. A tiny man trimming tiny rosebushes had a price sticker that said $189.95.

After I had put all the ornaments back in their tissue paper I sat on the laundry tiles and stared at the boxes. For the first time in two months my brain wasn't imagining anything. I sat there until Mum opened the door.

She looked at me, and then she looked at the boxes, and then she said, "What are you doing?"

"Looking for the big umbrella," I said.

"I moved it," she said, and then she closed the cupboard doors. "It's in the spare room. I'll get it for you." She went out for a minute and came back with the umbrella. She gave it to me without asking what I was going to do with it or where I thought I was going in this weather. I didn't say anything, and I didn't move. Mum twisted her hair around her finger the way she does when something is making her uncomfortable, like a horror movie or talking to her sister-in-law. She knew I was waiting for some kind of explanation.

Finally she said, "Your dad did some shopping."

And then she went back to the kitchen.

TWENTY-ONE

I WAS SITTING ON MY OWN BY the monkey bars when Rhea Grimm came up to me. I wasn't eating my lunch because I didn't know exactly what it was (it smelled like a cross between spaghetti sauce and pineapple) and I wasn't hungry. Even though I was trying harder than ever not to think, my brain was asking lots of questions and answering none of them. The main questions my brain kept asking were:

1. Why did my dad need so many ornaments?
2. What didn't I understand about Grandpa?
3. What exactly was Buddhism?
4. Where were the peacocks?

Because I was thinking all these thoughts I didn't see

Rhea Grimm until she was halfway across the handball courts. By then it was too late to do anything except scrunch up small and pretend to be studying my shoes and hope it wasn't me she was pounding across the asphalt toward.

"Hey. Andersen."

It was.

When I looked up, Rhea Grimm and three other Year Eight girls were standing in front of me. They all had messy buns with bits of hair dangling off them, and lots of jewelry. They all looked angry, but Rhea Grimm looked the angriest. Even with makeup her face was red. She had both hands on her hips, and—even though it was lunchtime and not home time—she had her schoolbag over her shoulder. She was standing so close to me that the bottom of her school dress almost touched my nose, and every time she spoke little bits of angry spit landed in my hair.

"Me?" My voice was more mouse than person.

"Yeah, you."

Rhea Grimm's friends giggled the way mean kids do when they have pulled the wings off a bug and are watching it try to fly away. But Rhea Grimm didn't even smile, and that was when I knew she wasn't just angry. She was furious. "Guess what?" she said.

"What?" I squeaked. A big part of me was wishing

more than anything that they would walk back across the handball courts and find some other bug to torture. But the part of me that was still a detective wanted to know what Rhea Grimm was so furious about.

"I'm suspended," she said. "Guess who suspended me?"

I swallowed and didn't say anything. I didn't need to guess.

"Your dad," Rhea Grimm said. "Your crazy, psycho, loser dad."

I stayed quiet. It felt like I had fallen down a very dark, very deep hole. But what really frightened me about this hole wasn't the dark, or the deep. It was the feeling I had that The Truth was sitting at the bottom of it with me.

Rhea Grimm's friends started to get even closer, like seagulls closing in on dropped chips at the beach.

"And you know what else?" Rhea Grimm leaned down and spoke straight into my face. "You know what he did right before he told me to get out?" Her voice crackled like something burning. "He cried. He sat down at his desk and cried. Like a baby. You know what happens when dads cry, don't you, Andersen?"

I didn't know, but I had a bad feeling. At the back of Rhea Grimm's eyes, behind her anger, I could see a little bit of happiness that came from making me sad.

"What happens?" I said.

"They go away," Rhea Grimm said. "They go away, and they don't come back."

And that was when I knew I wasn't just in a hole with The Truth: I was sitting right in the middle of it, and it was damp and sticky and bad-smelling. Tears were heating up the backs of my eyes and I knew I would only be able to hold them in for about three more seconds before I sobbed in Rhea Grimm's face. Just like she said my dad had done.

But then, from behind Rhea Grimm, there was a different voice. And the different voice said, "Did you know—"

Rhea Grimm turned around. I could see her pink polka-dot knickers peeking out from under her dress.

"—if you mix peanut butter and tomato sauce together it smells really, really bad. And—"

Rhea Grimm's friends moved back, and I saw Jonas standing there with two water balloons in each hand.

"—it stains really, really well."

Then there were four loud smacking sounds, like play-dough being thrown on a tile floor, and screaming. Lots of screaming. Rhea Grimm and her friends ran like it was sports day and they were doing the hundred meters. Just before Rhea Grimm disappeared behind the lockers I noticed something red-brown running down her front. I knew Jonas was good at science and facts, but I didn't know he was such a good shot.

"I saw them coming," Jonas said, and he sat down next

to me. "I've had the balloons in my locker for a while. Science experiment."

"A while?" I said.

Jonas smiled in a lopsided sort of way. "Three weeks."

We laughed because we were both thinking the same thing, and that thing was Rhea Grimm covered in three-week-old peanut butter and tomato sauce. And then we sat quietly together. I was thinking about The Truth, and Jonas was thinking about the day he had followed my dad into The Clinic and we stopped being friends.

"I didn't really see anything," Jonas said. "Just the waiting room. Your dad was reading a newspaper, and then the lady at the front desk called his name and he went into another room. That's all. Cross my heart."

I nodded. Jonas telling me what he saw didn't make me feel better, but it did feel true. And The Truth of what Jonas and Rhea Grimm had said was so heavy that I couldn't hold it up anymore. When I let it go I felt like a balloon slowly running out of air: sighing, soft and empty.

On my way home from school I saw William Shakespeare. He was standing on top of the little hill behind the church, watching me. He had lost all of his blue-green feathers and when he opened his tail I could see through it to the blank, empty sky behind him. He wasn't that far away but I was so tired that I couldn't even imagine walking up the hill, let alone *actually* walking up it. As I turned the corner away from William Shakespeare I heard him cry out, but the sound of him didn't make me feel anything. I wondered if I even wanted to be a peacock detective anymore.

At dinner I couldn't look straight at my dad. Everything he did seemed strange and sad. The way he stirred his borscht around in circles, the way he sat with his shoulders pulled down, the way he stared at Mum with a hypnotized look on his face, like she was a lava lamp. When he asked me how school was all I could think of was Rhea Grimm's face, and I looked down at my prosciutto-and-cheese tart like it was a really interesting bug under a microscope.

In between dinner and dessert Dad went to his study and Diana went to her room and Mum and I were in the kitchen alone. I was sitting on the couch pretending to watch TV but really thinking about Rhea Grimm. Mum fiddled around behind the counter for a while. The dishes were done and dessert was already made, so she sort of just moved plates and cups around for no real reason. Eventually she said, "Cassie, can you turn that off, please? I want to talk to you for a minute."

I switched off the news, and Mum came and sat next to me. She pushed her hair back behind her ears and licked her lips before she spoke.

"I've got a job," she said. There was some silence. "At

Calpurnia's. They've asked me to help out in the kitchen. Salads and desserts, mostly. I start next week."

Calpurnia's is the name of The Very Nice Restaurant on The Other Side of Town.

"That's good," I said. "Congratulations."

"Thank you." Mum pulled a strand of hair from behind her ear and started playing with it. "There's something else. I'm not going to be living here anymore. I'm moving out."

This time the silence was so strong and solid it felt like stone.

"To the backyard?" I said.

Mum shook her head. "No. To my own place. For a while."

I tried to imagine good reasons for my mum moving out. Like her being a lion tamer with a traveling circus, or a secret superhero, or the prime minister. But none of these reasons were true enough, and I didn't believe any of them.

"Cassie?" Mum was looking at me very carefully. "Are you all right?"

"What about Dad and Diana?" I said. "What will they say?"

Mum took a deep breath. "I've already told them," she said. "They understand. Cassie . . ." She stopped and looked down at her hand—the one with her wedding ring—and then back at me. "It's difficult to explain. But this is really important to me. Does that make sense?"

I nodded, even though it didn't make any sense at all, because I was starting to feel dizzy and I didn't trust myself to speak.

Mum smiled, and hugged me. "I love you," she said, into my hair. When she pulled back her eyes had tears in them. "All right. Dessert?"

Dad and Diana came back and we sat down at the table with little bowls of pink mousse. I waited for someone to say something about Mum's news, but no one did. Diana was sitting perfectly still, the way she does when she's Meditating, and her eyes were staring far off into the distance. Dad was looking down at his lap, where he was twisting a napkin around his fingers. That made me really mad, because I thought my dad really loved my mum, but now she was going to leave and Dad was acting like he didn't even care. So because Diana was Meditating and Dad was twisting, I was the only one who could say something to Mum.

And what I said was, "You can't leave."

Mum put down her spoon. "Possum," she said. "Try to look on the bright side. I'll still see you every day, and you can come and stay with me whenever you like."

But I didn't want to look on the bright side. "I don't want to stay with you. I want you to stay here."

"I know this is difficult, Cassie, but when you're older you'll understand."

"I understand a lot of things now." I stood up. "Like what's in an R-rated movie, and how to swear in Greek, and what sausages are made of. And I want to understand why you don't want to live with us anymore. I want to understand why Diana doesn't have to go to church and why she gets to live in the stupid backyard. I want to understand about Grandpa. And"— I turned my voice in Dad's direction —"I want to understand why you're not doing anything."

I was looking properly at Dad, which was something I hadn't done for months. He seemed smaller than usual, and grayer. "Say something," I said. But he didn't. "What's *wrong* with you?" I said.

Dad just kept twisting and twisting and twisting. And then—maybe because of all the twisting or because of Mum's news or Diana's Meditating or a whole lot of things mixed together—something I didn't know was in me started to rise up and grow, like a sickness or a sneeze. And that something made me do a thing I never thought I could do. I lifted my little bowl of pink mousse off the table, and dumped it upside down on top of Dad's head.

And then I left.

I didn't know I was walking to the bridge until I was already there.

I stopped in the middle, halfway between My Side and The Other Side of Town, and looked down at the water. All I could see were shiny bubbles where the rapids were catching the moonlight.

When I left, my only plan was to get away from home. But when I got to the bridge I realized home had followed me. My mind was full of Mum leaving, and Dad crying at school, and Diana staring into nothing. I tried to remember a time before home was so hard to think about: before Dad was going to The Clinic, and before Mum was cooking all the time, and before Diana was Meditating and being vegetarian and living outside. I tried remembering our Family Holiday, and how Diana and I had swum every day and Mum and Dad had held hands and we'd all played Scrabble. But now when I remembered it, everything was different. It had rained, and Diana and I had been bored, and Mum and Dad had argued about the price of Movie World tickets. Maybe Jonas was right: maybe family holidays *were* the worst, after all.

I thought if I stood and thought on the bridge for long enough I would feel better. Usually if I think really carefully I can take the things that are making me feel bad and turn them into something that has meaning. Like a story. But when I started to try to give all these thoughts transition words and paragraphs it didn't feel right. And it didn't feel right because it didn't feel true.

After a while I gave up and went to find some sticks to throw off the bridge. There were some good ones just near the road, at the edge of the track. I threw them into the water on one side of the bridge and then I ran to the other side to see which one was the winner. That's how you play Pooh Sticks, which is a game Diana and I have played together ever since we moved to Bloomsbury. I had to squint to see the sticks in the dark, and it wasn't much fun since both sticks were mine so I always won. But I kept playing because finding sticks and throwing them and running and squinting was better than just standing and thinking.

I threw two sticks in and ran across the bridge. But when I looked down three sticks came out. I turned around, and that's when I saw someone standing on the stick-throwing side of the bridge. That someone was Diana. She found me partly because she likes to play Pooh Sticks on the bridge (or she did before she was fifteen), but mostly because she is my sister.

For a few seconds we had to stand and look at each other—her on the stick-throwing side and me on the stick-looking side—because a car went between us. And it was when the headlights of the car shone on Diana's face that I knew something was wrong. Not just me-dumping-pink-mousse-on-Dad's-head-and-leaving sort of wrong. Something else.

We met each other in the middle of the road, which is a dangerous thing to do but right then it didn't matter. When I got close to Diana I could see she was crying and so I started crying too, because if Diana cries I cry, and that's just how it is. It's like how dogs always wag their tails when they see someone they love. They can't help it.

We stood in the middle of the road crying and hugging for ages, and I didn't know why we were doing any of this. But then Diana wiped her eyes and sniffed and stopped enough to say, "Grandpa's in hospital."

First I thought she meant Grandpa was *at* the hospital because someone he knew was sick and he was visiting them. It made no sense for Diana to say that Grandpa was *in* hospital, since Grandpa was always doing things for other people and not for himself. So I thought that Diana had got her prepositions (which is the kind of words that *at* and *in* are) confused. But then I realized we wouldn't be standing in the middle of the road crying if Grandpa was just *at* the hospital visiting somebody we didn't even know. And then I realized what Diana really meant but didn't have the breath to say was: "Grandpa's really sick. So sick that he's in hospital. Which means he doesn't have a cold or the flu or a tummy bug. Which means he has something serious. Which means we have to stand here and hug each other and cry in the middle of the road even though it's dark and even though it's dangerous, because we don't know what else to do."

And when I realized The Truth about why we were crying I also realized that there was no way to fix it. Thinking differently couldn't fix it, and finding the peacocks couldn't fix it, and Metaphors couldn't fix it. Not even writing this story could make The Truth better. And I looked at Diana and she nodded, and I knew she knew exactly what I was thinking.

We stayed like that in the road for a long time, until a car came, and we had to move.

PART TWO

Winter

TWENTY-TWO

LAST YEAR FOR MY GRADE FIVE CULTURE project, I learned about Hinduism. Hinduism is a religion from India, and it has a different kind of Creation Story. In Hinduism, God has three parts. The first part is called Brahma. Brahma is the creator, which means he made the universe and the planets and the grass and the caterpillars. The second part is Vishnu. Vishnu looks after everything that Brahma made.

The third part is Shiva. Shiva destroys everything that has been made and looked after by Brahma and Vishnu. He breaks it into pieces and stomps on it—all the planets and the grass and the caterpillars—like a little kid having a tantrum. He kills people and animals, too—even dogs that never did anything to anyone. The bit about Shiva is not really a Creation Story. It is a Destruction Story.

I never used to like Shiva's story. I didn't understand why someone would exist just to destroy things. And I didn't understand why people in India built temples and wrote stories and made art for Shiva. I thought Brahma and Vishnu were the good guys, and Shiva was bad.

But now Shiva's story makes sense to me, and it makes sense because it is true. And it is true because in real life nothing lasts forever. In real life people move out and turn fifteen and get sick. In real life The Truth is things getting broken and stomped on. And any story that tells you something different is A Lie.

Winter came quickly. At the end of autumn it was chilly, but as soon as the calendar turned over to June it was cold. And now that it's July it is freezing. Winter in Bloomsbury looks like snow on the mountains and darkness at five o'clock. It sounds like blackbirds sitting in leafless trees going *caw caw . . . caaawww*. It feels like frost. It tastes like frost. It smells like frost. Winter is like a giant mud puddle in the middle of the road with no way around it. You know you need to get to the other side, but you also know you will have to get your feet wet.

In June Mum moved into a flat. The Flat is all the way past Lee Street, on The Other Side of Town. Mum says it is "very cozy" but I think it is just very small. Mum and Dad made a deal that when Mum has nights off from The Very Nice Restaurant Diana and I stay with her at The Flat. So on Tuesdays and Wednesdays we pack clean clothes and homework and toothbrushes and towels and walk across the bridge. Diana isn't allowed to sleep outside at The Flat since the only outside Mum has is a courtyard that is mostly cold concrete. So Diana sleeps on the floor in the living room/kitchen and I sleep on the foldout couch in the living room/kitchen. The foldout couch is hard and cold, and the walls and curtains are all cream-colored ("I've always wanted cream-colored curtains," Mum said when she moved in, but I've never heard her want them before). So when I stay at The Flat I feel like I'm in a fridge and I can't sleep. When Mum moved there she asked me if I wanted to live with her full-time. I said, "No, thanks," because even though I was still angry with Dad I was worried about him, too. I thought leaving him alone in the house was a bad idea.

One day in June I was walking home from school when Tom Golding started walking next to me. But he didn't smile and say, "Hi, Cassie." Instead, he sighed and said, "Why doesn't Diana talk to me anymore?"

His mouth was straight and thin, like those mechanical pencil leads that always break.

"She's Meditating," I said. "She's finding a place where she doesn't need anything." But I don't think this was the right answer, because Tom Golding turned around and walked back the way he had already come, and didn't even say, "See ya, Cassie."

Dad is having more of Those Days. He had so many in a row that he stopped going to work, and now he just sits on the couch in his pajamas and watches TV. He is using his long service leave, which he was supposed to be saving for our next Family Holiday. He stopped going to The Clinic, too. The only times he ever goes out are to visit Grandpa in the hospital, or to buy more boxes. There are so many boxes now that Dad has started filling the kitchen cupboards with them.

Once a week Diana takes Dad's wallet and goes to the supermarket to buy milk and bread and other groceries. Most nights we eat food from Tupperware containers that Mum drops off on her way to work, but sometimes Diana cooks. Diana only knows how to cook two things:

1. Spaghetti with tomato sauce, and
2. Toasted cheese sandwiches.

I used to really like both of these things, but after eating them every week for a month and a half I don't like them so much anymore. When Diana isn't cooking she is cleaning, or helping me with my math homework. She is also trying really hard not to get angry at Dad. (I can tell because sometimes when she looks at him her calm face disappears for a second and is replaced by a frustrated-and-tired face.)

William Shakespeare's feathers that I found are starting

to look droopy. I haven't seen the peacocks since the end of May, when William Shakespeare yelled at me from the hill. Not-seeing the peacocks is a problem because this story is supposed to be about losing peacocks and looking for peacocks and finding peacocks. I'm worried that if the peacocks aren't in this story anymore you will stop reading and will find something more interesting to do instead, like making biscuits or bike riding or going to the cinema. Thinking about nobody reading this story makes it even harder to write.

We visit Grandpa in the hospital every day after school, and on weekends. Except I don't really visit, because Mum says I shouldn't see Grandpa Like That. I don't know what Like That means, except it has something to do with being very sick. When I ask Dad what Grandpa looks like he just says, "Different." So I sit outside Grandpa's room in the hospital hallway while Dad and Diana go inside. While I'm sitting there I try to imagine how Grandpa could look so bad that he wouldn't want me to see him. Then I test myself to see if I really wouldn't want to see him if he looked that way. I imagine him with long nails and hair, and teeth like a wolf. But I still want to see him. I imagine him with blood coming out his ears and black lips and a really fat stomach and even then I still want to see him. I imagine a thousand different, horrible Grandpas. But none of them is horrible enough. I still want to see him. And I'm still not allowed to.

TWENTY-THREE

JONAS AND I ARE FRIENDS AGAIN AND we sit together every lunchtime at school. Even though it's winter I still sit on the other side of the footpath. I know—because it is a fact—that the snake is hibernating. But I still feel in my stomach like the snake is wide awake and waiting under the stairs to strike at my ankles.

Jonas will be twelve on the 30th of July, but he isn't excited. When I showed Jonas the birthday party invitation his mum had put in our letter box he told me to throw it out. He says he doesn't want a party, and that the 30th of July isn't his real birthday. When I asked him when his real birthday is he just scuffed his feet on the steps and glared.

Jonas still tells me facts but now most of his facts are

interesting-and-disturbing. For example: "Did you know that tapeworms can live in your intestines and eat all the food you eat and get stronger while you get weaker?" I still tell Jonas stories, too, except now all the stories I tell are true and most of them are sad. Because we are both already feeling bad we like to hear sad stories and disturbing facts. It's funny how when you feel bad you want to do things that make you feel worse. It's like feeling worse makes you feel better, somehow.

Today I told Jonas a true story about Akela. Akela was my dog who died when I was seven years old. Akela had been in our family since before Diana and I were born. I showed Jonas a photo of me and Akela. In the photo I am only one year old and Akela is much bigger than me. She is all black except for her stomach and under her chin, which is white and tufty. Her fur sticks out like a lion's mane. One of my hands is grabbing onto Akela's fur and I am staring at her. My eyes are really big and my mouth is open like I can't believe she exists. Akela is looking at the camera. She doesn't have her mouth open, or her tongue out, and she is not smiling. She looks more serious in this photo than some people ever look. She is saying—with her eyes and her white mane—"If you try to hurt this baby I will kill you. I will really, properly, kill you." When Grandpa got sick I took this photo out of its frame on top of the microwave and put it in my bag.

I told Jonas that when Akela died she was sixteen years

old, which is almost one hundred in dog years. We knew she was going to die because she stopped eating, and she didn't want to go for walks or bark at people walking past our house anymore. Most of the time before Akela died she just lay down wherever people were. (When Akela got old she was allowed to be an inside dog.) If we were having dinner she would lie next to the table, but she wasn't waiting for leftovers like Simon does. If we were watching TV she would lie in front of the couch with her head on Mum's feet. And sometimes when Mum and Dad and Diana were in the living room and I was in my bedroom reading, Akela would come and lie on my floor. When she did that I felt really, really special.

I told Jonas how Akela had died on a school day. When Diana and I got home Mum was waiting for us in the kitchen. She said Akela was really sick and had to be Put Down.

"First when Mum said Put Down I didn't understand what she meant," I yelled (not too loudly) to Jonas. "But then Mum explained that when vets say Put Down it means something else. She said when vets say Put Down what they really mean is kill."

Jonas nodded. "It's a euphemism," he yelled (softly).

"What's that?" I yelled (softly) back.

"It's a word that makes something horrible seem not-so-bad. Like saying casualties instead of people killed in war, or laid off instead of sacked." (Jonas doesn't just know facts about science; he knows facts about words, too. This is another reason why we are friends.)

"That's a sad story," Jonas yelled when I was finished. And by sad story I knew he meant good story. "Do you want to know an interesting-and-disturbing fact about sandflies?"

There was one part of the story about Akela that I didn't tell Jonas. And that was how after Mum had told me and Diana about the vet I went to my room. In my room I pretended to be a worm, busy wriggling, buried in warm dirt. And while I was pretending Mum came in and looked in my cupboard for something, and then she turned around and hugged me and she was crying. That was the first time I ever saw my mum cry. I didn't tell Jonas this part because talking about it makes me scared. It makes me scared the same way Dad taking long service leave so he can sit at home all day makes me scared. It makes me feel like I am big, and Mum and Dad are small. Which is wrong because I'm eleven-turning-twelve and Mum and Dad are old-turning-older. It is weird and disturbing, like tapeworms. Or like someone saying Put Down when they really mean kill.

TWENTY-FOUR

TODAY WAS A SORT-OF-SUNNY WINTER DAY, SO after not-visiting Grandpa I went to lie in the grass outside Diana's tent.

After I had been lying there a little while Diana said, "He's not getting better, you know."

I wasn't reading anything. I was just lying and looking down at the grass. It rained yesterday, and the ground was damp. When Diana said what she said, I was watching a worm. I liked the way it wandered around in its fragile body. So small, and so squishable.

"How do you know?" I said. Being fifteen means you know more things, like trigonometry and art history, but it doesn't mean you know everything.

"He's been sick for ages," Diana said.

"Only since June," I said. "That's not ages."

"He's been in hospital since June. He's been sick since Christmas."

I stopped looking at bugs. At Christmas we had gone to Aunt Sally's, like always. We had eaten turkey and pudding, like always. Grandpa had sat on the veranda and done crosswords, like always. And then we had come home.

"No, he wasn't," I said. "We went to Aunt Sally's."

"Grandpa wanted to go. He wanted Christmas to be normal," said Diana.

I tried remembering Christmas again. We had gone to Aunt Sally's, like always. We had eaten turkey, but Grandpa hadn't had any pudding. We hadn't sung Christmas carols like we always did—instead we had watched TV. And Grandpa had started a lot of crosswords, but he hadn't finished any of them.

Then I remembered coming home from Christmas. I remembered Dad having more of Those Days, and Mum cooking all the time, and Diana Meditating and not going to church. And that was when I realized I was remembering The Truth about Christmas, and that everything I had remembered before was A Lie.

"How come no one told me?" I said.

"You're too young, Cassie," Diana said. "You wouldn't have understood."

I was getting really sick of people telling me this. Mum, Dad, teachers, Ms. Carol the librarian, who won't let me take out books from the high school section even though I can read at a Year Seven level. I was so sick of hearing this sentence that I didn't know what to say. I just lay in the grass and watched the worm trying to push its way into a clump of mud.

"Cassie . . ." Diana looked down at her book like she wanted to be reading it but couldn't. She folded and unfolded the bottom corner of the page. "I heard Mrs. Harris talking to Dad this afternoon. She said there's not much else they can do. Except make him comfortable."

"Comfortable?" I said this word like it was from a language I don't understand, like Russian. "How can he be comfortable if he's dying?"

Diana just looked at me.

"Comfortable is reading a book in the sun, or watching a movie in a beanbag with popcorn. Dying is no more sun, no more books, no more popcorn. Dying is the end of everything. How can that be comfortable?"

I didn't really expect Diana to answer this question, and she didn't. She looked down at her book.

"You don't really mean comfortable," I said. "Comfortable is a euphemism. What you really mean is giving up. What you really mean is doing nothing and letting Grandpa die."

Diana looked up. Her eyes were like tadpoles swimming in tears. I could tell she was waiting for me to say something nice, something that would make her feel better. Something that would make both of us feel better. But I didn't want to be nice.

I stood up. "You shouldn't lie like that, Diana," I said. Then I stomped back to the house. I felt bad because it was a pretty mean thing to say to someone I really loved very much. And when I got to the deck and bent over to take off my shoes I felt even worse, because I realized I had squashed the worm.

I'm going to tell you something that I've never told anyone, not even my dad. Some days I don't want to write anything at all. Not even this story. Some days when I look at this notebook on the dresser next to William Shakespeare's feathers I feel sick right down deep in my stomach. I want to do anything that isn't writing. Anything. Even eating chard or working out multiplication problems.

The reason I can't say this to anyone—especially not my dad—is because everyone thinks I'm a Writer. When Dad introduces me to new people he says, "This is my daughter Cassie. She's writing a book." At church Grandpa says to his friends, "My granddaughter writes the most wonderful stories." At school Mrs. Atkinson takes time out from doing important work like The Budget to read my stories. Even Mum says to people, "Cassie's definitely got Mark's imagination." Whenever anybody I know thinks about me the thought in their head looks like this:

Cassie = Writer

And if I told people that some days I hate writing, the thought in their heads when they think of me would look like this:

Cassie =

Which is a very unbalanced thought, and it makes me feel like I'm sitting on a seesaw with no one at the other end.

Sometimes I think about changing this equation so that when people think of me they see something else on the other side of the equals sign instead of Writer. Like:

Cassie = Scientist

or

Cassie = Chef

or

Cassie = High Jump Champion

But none of those things seems right. And I wonder if I will ever find something that really fits, or if I will just grow up being half a person pretending to be something I'm not.

TWENTY-FIVE

TODAY MUM TURNED FORTY SO SHE TOOK me and Diana to The Very Nice Restaurant to celebrate. She wore a black dress and stockings and the pearl earrings Dad gave her for their anniversary last year. I thought it was unfair to wear Dad's earrings to a dinner he wasn't invited to, so I tried not to look at Mum's ears. This probably would have made Mum mad if she hadn't been so distracted by Roger.

Diana and I couldn't get dressed up for The Very Nice Restaurant because we had forgotten to pack our nice clothes. We had to wear our school uniforms, which are just blue dresses without any shape and black shoes without heels. I could tell Mum wanted to blame Dad for us not having nice clothes because she made a face when she saw what was in our bags like she had just eaten a bad potato chip (one that is green at the edges instead of crispy yellow). But she didn't say anything. She just plaited our hair—hard—and then put in her earrings.

When we got to The Very Nice Restaurant, Roger was waiting for us at the door. He kissed Mum on the cheek and said, "How's it going, kids?" to me and Diana (which I knew made Diana mad because now that she is fifteen she hates being called a kid).

I guess Roger is all-right-looking from the outside. He is tall and straight. His nose is a nice shape and his chin has an almost-beard that is always trimmed very neatly. His clothes are never wrinkled and they look like they come from somewhere more expensive than Target. But there is something a bit wobbly about Roger. Looking at him sometimes reminds me of looking at a mirage on a hot day—he is sort of shimmering. Like he might come apart and disappear any minute. When he showed us our table he pulled Mum's chair out for her, and the way he smiled reminded me of the Cheshire Cat in *Alice in Wonderland*.

I wanted to order spaghetti but there wasn't any on the menu. The closest thing (Mum said) was Chicken Linguine with Cream Sauce and Shaved Truffles. The only thing I know about truffles is that they come from underground and you have to use a pig to find them. So I said I would have that, because then I could imagine a pig snorting and snuffling and digging up the truffles for my dinner. Diana said she wasn't hungry. Mum said she had to eat anyway, and then she waved to Roger and he came over to our table.

"I'll have the Barramundi," Mum said. "Cassandra will have the Chicken Linguine with Truffles." (Mum only calls me Cassandra when she is angry with me or when she is trying to sound fancy.) "Diana?"

"A garden salad, please," Diana said, in her polite voice. "And some more bread." As soon as Roger walked away Mum turned to Diana with scrunched eyebrows.

"That was very rude."

"What?" Diana asked (and she was really asking, not being fifteen and sarcastic).

"You don't ask for more bread in a place like this," Mum said. "It's insulting."

"Insulting to who?"

"To the chef."

"Why? It's delicious bread," Diana said. She took a big bite of her baguette. Bits of crust scattered all over the table.

Roger spent more time at our table than he did at any of the others. I know because I was timing him. The time he spent looked like this:

Family of four by the window: two minutes, eight
    seconds.
Romantic couple by the fireplace: one minute,
    forty seconds.
Big group of laughing old people with lots of
    wine: one minute, fifty-two seconds.
Our table: seven minutes, twenty-two seconds.

After Roger had finished spending six minutes, thirty-eight seconds talking to Mum about salad dressings and had gone back to the kitchen I asked, "Why does Roger spend so much time at our table?"

Mum had a sip of her wine. "He wants to make sure we have a nice dinner. That's his job."

"What about everyone else?" Diana said. "Doesn't he want to make sure they have nice dinners, too?"

Mum twisted a piece of hair around her fingers. "He's looking after us a bit more because I work here. We're friends."

Diana was looking at Mum the way detectives look at possible suspects. "You must be very good friends," she said.

Mum put down her wineglass. "Diana," she said, in her warning voice.

"What?" Diana said, and this time she *was* being fifteen and sarcastic. She picked up another piece of bread. "I'm just saying."

I waited for Mum to tell Diana to stop eating bread, but she didn't. She just stared at Diana until Roger came over with our food.

We ate in silence, and I couldn't enjoy the truffles that the pig had snuffled out for me. And later when Diana and I were lying together in the cold, white living room/kitchen I wanted more than anything to talk to her. But I didn't, because we were still in a fight, and because I didn't know how to begin.

On Saturday I decided—even though it was cold and damp outside—that Simon needed a walk. Since it became winter Simon hasn't been for many walks at all. This is partly because it's too cold, but mostly because Mum isn't home and Dad is always watching TV and Diana is always cooking and cleaning and doing homework. So the only person left to go walking with Simon this morning was me.

I was also feeling guilty about the peacocks. I hadn't seen them all winter, and I hoped they were okay and not too cold. I also hoped that the reason I hadn't found them yet was because they were really good at hiding. But deep down I knew it was really because I wasn't looking hard enough.

We walked down to the river and along the track. The wind felt like ice, and there was snow on the very tops of the mountains so they looked like they were wearing white elf hats. Simon was still sniffing everything, but because the ground was so damp grass kept sticking to his nose and he had to stop every two minutes to sneeze it off. We got to the bridge and I was about to turn us left to visit Jonas when Virginia appeared out of the bush.

She stood in the middle of the bridge and looked at us. She seemed smaller, standing on the smooth, wide road. Her feathers were dark from the damp.

She bobbed her head. Simon barked. Virginia squawked, and then she turned and ran away from us across the bridge. Simon barked again and we followed.

Simon was running fast and I was concentrating so hard on not letting go of his lead that I didn't notice where we were heading until we were already there. Then we stopped and looked and where we were was The Other Side of Town, past Lee Street, outside Mum's Flat. Virginia flapped herself over the back fence and was gone.

Between the front and back of The Flat there is a little path behind a gate that I am just tall enough to open if I stand on my tiptoes. Simon and I squeezed our way down the little path past the air conditioner and into the backyard. The backyard is really just a concrete square with a barbecue and a clothesline and some herbs in pots that Mum uses for cooking. There is nowhere for a peacock to hide in Mum's backyard, but Virginia had disappeared.

I sighed and Simon growled. I thought about knocking on the back door and asking Mum if she had seen where Virginia went, but I knew if I did that she would ask me questions about school and Diana and Dad that I didn't feel like answering. Instead, Simon and I sat down behind the barbecue for a rest. Chasing peacocks (especially Virginia) makes you really tired.

The back door of The Flat is the kind of door that slides and is made of glass. This was why, while Simon and I were sitting there catching our breath behind the barbecue, we could see into the kitchen. And it was why we could see that on the counter were chopped-up tomatoes and cheese and those long green onions that are fun to sprinkle on things—all ingredients for making an omelette. And it was why we could see someone standing at the counter, wearing pajamas and mixing eggs in a bowl. And that someone we saw was not my mum. That someone was Roger.

When my eyes saw Roger my brain asked three questions in this order:

1. Why is Roger making an omelette?
2. Why is Roger making an omelette in his pajamas?
3. Why is Roger making an omelette in his pajamas in my mum's kitchen?

As I pulled Simon around the corner and back down

the side-path my brain answered all three questions at once. And then it put those answers together with all the Tupperware in our freezer with Roger's name on it, and Diana looking at Mum strangely at dinner at The Very Nice Restaurant. And then it told me The Truth.

"Roger is your mum's boyfriend," my brain said. "She wants to always be around him. She wants to eat omelettes with him, and hug him, and kiss him. One day she'll want to marry him. And there's nothing you can do about it."

Simon and I ran back to the bridge, which seemed like a safe distance from The Flat. When we got there we stopped. I didn't want to go home, because going home would mean seeing Dad's face and I didn't know if I could see Dad's face after seeing Roger's pajamas. So we didn't go anywhere. We just stood on the bridge, feeling like worms that had been dug out of warm earth and stomped on by someone's shoe.

We had to go home eventually, though, because Dad was waiting for me to go with him to the hospital. Diana was in her tent studying and I didn't want to sit in the car alone with Dad, so I tried to sneak Simon into the back seat. We were safe until just before Dad turned the key to start the car and Simon sneezed. (He still had some grass stuck to his nose from our walk.) Dad turned around.

"Out," he said, and Simon put his head down and crept out of the car and into the fernery. Dad looked at me like he wanted to be angry but all he could be was blank. He was wearing proper clothes, but he had on the face that he usually wears with his pajamas. "You can't bring a dog to a hospital," he said, in the sort of voice you use for things you should say (like spelling tests and Bible verses in church) and not things you want to say.

"Sorry," I said. I wanted to explain that it felt good to have Simon next to me because he was the only one who knew The Truth. But explaining this would mean also explaining Roger and the omelette, and that was something I couldn't do to my dad.

At the hospital I sat in the hallway while Dad went in to see Grandpa. I put my elbows on my knees and my chin in my hands and looked down at the floor, which was a sort of yellow-black color. It was the kind of floor that squeaked when you walked on it, like it was alive and you were hurting it with your shoes. It had no cracks in it like other floors did where bits of floor joined together, so it looked like a giant piece of spread-out skin. Yellow-black skin, like a tiger snake.

When Dad came out of Grandpa's room he still had his pajamas-face on. His sneakers were very rubbery and when he walked the floor sounded like it was screaming. I followed him, lifting my feet as high as I could. When we got to the doors we had to stop because Mum was walking in.

The floor went quiet because everyone stopped walking. I could tell from the way Mum's eyes went up and down and around and never stayed on Dad that she was thinking about Roger. She had a look on her face like there was a big shot put in her stomach.

"Mark," Mum said. Her voice was like a sigh. "How is he?"

Dad looked at me, and then at Mum. Mum nodded. I was half-annoyed that they were keeping a secret from me and half-happy that they were sharing a secret.

"How are you?" Dad said.

"Fine," Mum said.

"How's the restaurant?"

"Good." Mum twisted some hair around her finger. She said the word "good" like it was the word "tired."

"That's good," Dad said, and then, "Right." But there was nothing right about us all standing in the hallway of the hospital. There was nothing right about Grandpa being in a room all alone and me not being allowed to see him. And there was nothing right about the way Roger seemed to be hanging over the top of us, like a big saggy storm cloud looming closer and closer, about to hit Dad in the head.

"It's nice to see you, Helen," Dad said, and then he put

his head down and walked toward the automatic doors. They opened with a hiss, and he was gone.

Mum stopped me before I could follow him.

"Cassie, is everything okay?" Her eyes were so full of guilt they looked like a pot of boiling water about to overflow. And maybe it was because of the screaming floor or Grandpa just down the hall. Or maybe it was because it was just getting too hard to keep all this Truth inside me, that I said, "No." And then, "I hope it was a nice omelette."

And then I followed Dad through the snake-hiss doors.

TWENTY-SIX

AT SCHOOL TODAY JONAS WAS IN A really bad mood. He didn't tell me any facts (not even disturbing ones) and in science he wouldn't answer Mrs. Atkinson's questions about volcanoes (and Jonas knows a lot about volcanoes). At lunchtime he sat at the top of The Snake Stairs glaring and not-eating. When I yelled, "What's wrong?" he yelled back (unnecessarily loudly and angrily), "Nothing!"

And then a few seconds later, "Why do you have to sit all the way over there?"

I was sitting where I always sat, on the other side of the footpath, as far away from The Snake Stairs as I could get and still have a (loud) conversation.

"Because I'm scared of snakes," I yelled.

"I know," Jonas yelled. "But *why*?"

Here is a list of things I know about snakes:

1. They are cold-blooded, which means they need to lie in the sun to keep their bodies warm.

2. They use their tongues to smell and to figure out which way to go.

3. They can't hear but they can feel vibrations in the ground. (This is why it's important to stomp your feet when snakes might be around.)

4. They like to eat frogs and mice.

5. They don't take care of their babies.

6. There are lots of them in Victoria (which is the state Bloomsbury is in).

7. A lot of the snakes in Victoria are poisonous.

8. A lot of the poisonous snakes in Victoria are deadly.

9. In stories snakes are usually the bad guys (like in *The Jungle Book* and the Bible).

All of these are good reasons to be scared of snakes, but none of them is my reason. My reason is something that happened when I was little. I don't like telling people why I'm scared of snakes because even talking about it gives me goose bumps. I thought about how Jonas had seen the snake behind his house, and about how he had just stood there while the snake slid away, and about how he hadn't been scared. I thought maybe he wouldn't understand my reason. But then I remembered that Jonas is my friend and that he had saved me from Rhea Grimm, and I decided to tell him.

"Because of my dad," I said. "When I was six there was a tiger snake in our backyard. Diana was in the garden with Akela, and the snake came out from under the camellia bush. So Dad killed it."

Jonas was leaning forward so he could hear me. This was a story I didn't want to yell.

"What did it look like?" he asked.

"It was long," I said. "Longer than the shovel. And it was mostly black, but it had yellow stripes and a yellow tummy. Its neck was cut, and there was blood on the grass."

"Gross." Jonas said "gross" like he was saying "cool."

"Dad said it was dead. But—"

"But what?" Jonas was leaning so far forward I thought he was going to fall off the steps.

"It was moving. Its tail was moving. And its mouth and eyes were open."

"Things can be dead and still have their eyes open," Jonas said.

"Yeah, but they weren't just open. They were looking."

"Looking at what?"

"At my dad."

There was some silence then, because I had stopped telling the story.

"Then what happened?" Jonas said.

"Nothing," I said. "That's the end."

Jonas sat back on the stairs. "That's not a very good story."

I shrugged. My feelings were a bit hurt, but I knew Jonas was in a bad mood and when people are in bad moods sometimes they say things they don't mean. I also felt guilty because I had lied to Jonas when I said that was the end. There were two things about my snake story that I hadn't told him:

1. After I saw the snake with its eyes open I screamed so loud that Mr. and Mrs. Hudson heard me from across the road, and

2. I didn't just see the snake looking at my dad. I saw the snake looking at my dad like it would kill him. Not just like it *wanted* to kill him, but like it actually, definitely, would kill him. As actually and definitely as the sun.

TWENTY-SEVEN

TODAY WAS JONAS'S BIRTHDAY BUT HE WASN'T at school. He wasn't there for math, or Japanese. I looked for him on The Snake Stairs at lunchtime to give him his present, but he wasn't there either.

When I got home Dad was sitting at the kitchen table with his glasses on, and Peter and Irene were sitting next to him. Irene is usually very pretty and friendly looking, with her curly brown hair and round cheeks. Peter is usually smiling and stroking his chin while he tells science jokes, like: "What do molecules say when they wake up in the morning? Up and atom!" But today Irene had big red eyes and Peter had the most serious face I had ever seen, like someone was pulling the corners of his mouth with string to make it straight. When I came in they all stood up and seeing them standing there with their faces like that made me want to go straight to my room.

"Cassandra," Dad said, so I knew right away something was really wrong. "Have you seen Jonas?"

The shot-put feeling started building in my stomach. Because I hadn't seen him. Not in class and not on The Snake Stairs.

"No," I said.

"When was the last . . ." Irene started speaking but her voice was really shaky and she had to stop before she was done. Peter finished her sentence for her.

"When was the last time you saw him?" he said.

"Yesterday," I said. "At school. We had music last and then we got our bags and I walked home and Jonas walked home."

"Which way?" Irene's voice was like a peacock's, high and sad. "Which way did he go?"

"The same way he always goes," I said. "Left, past the church, and home."

Irene's eyes watered. Peter's mouth got so straight I couldn't see his lips anymore.

"Jonas didn't come home after school yesterday," Peter said. It was a sentence that didn't make sense to me because Jonas always went home after school. He didn't play football or basketball, and he didn't have any friends to visit. He always went home because at home were the things he liked to do. For example, going on the internet and reading his encyclopedias.

"Cassie, do you have any idea where he might be?"

I was thinking about Jonas the last time I had seen him. How he had been angry and quiet, not telling me any facts or answering any questions or even once talking about his birthday. I was wondering when Jonas had decided to leave. Had he known on Monday morning he was leaving? In science? All through spelling? While we were eating lunch on The Snake Stairs?

"Cassie, please." Peter's voice was desperate, like a dog crying at a locked back door.

"I don't know," I said.

"Cassandra." Dad's voice was a warning.

"Really. Cross my heart," I said. Then Irene cried. Peter put his arm around her. Dad just stood there looking sad and uncomfortable. I imagined Jonas at the school gate, with his bag, knowing he was leaving but not saying anything. Just waving like he always did and turning away. I had thought Jonas was my friend who trusted me and told me everything. But now I was starting to think that The Truth was something different.

For dinner Diana said we could get takeout, so I put on my coat to walk to the fish-and-chip shop with her. Diana picked up Dad's wallet off the bench and looked inside it. Then she went into the kitchen and started getting stuff out of the fridge for toasted cheese sandwiches.

"What are you doing?" I said.

"What does it look like," Diana said, without a question mark because she didn't really want an answer.

"We had toasted cheese last night."

"Just set the table."

I knew from Diana's tone (which was tired and grumpy with a little bit of sad mixed in) that the conversation was over, so I got out the tablecloth and the water glasses and the tomato sauce. It took me a while to find the tomato sauce because now the pantry was half-full of boxes, too.

I was sitting on the couch with Dad watching the news (they were talking about a bomb that had exploded in London) when the house phone rang. Diana was toasting cheese and Dad isn't good with phones when he's having Those Days, so I answered it.

"Hello, this is Cassie speaking."

"Cassie." It was Mum. Hearing her voice made something inside me go soft, like melting ice cream. But then I remembered that I was still mad at her about Roger and the omelette. I forced my insides to freeze up again.

"Hello," I said, in the most formal, frozen voice I have.

"How are you?" Mum said.

"Fine."

The TV said: "Evil act of terror."

"What are you having for dinner?"

"Toasted cheese."

"Again? Put your sister on."

I held out the phone to Diana.

The TV said: "Person of interest."

Diana turned off the stove and took the phone.

"Yeah?" she said, which is definitely not the way Mum taught us to answer the phone. There was a pause so Mum could yell at Diana for answering the phone like that. Then Diana said, "I'm making dinner. I have to go." Then she hung up. The color of Diana's face told me that Mum hadn't finished her side of the conversation.

The TV said: "Incomprehensible."

I wasn't hungry. With all the worry about Jonas in my stomach there wasn't room for food. I picked off some of the crusts and nibbled a little bit of cheese that was leaking out the edges. Dad took his sandwich into his study and shut the door. Before he went he mumbled, "Thanks, sweetheart," to Diana. She just glared at him and gave him his wallet.

Diana let me leave the table early, even though I hadn't really eaten anything. If Mum had been there she would have made me sit at the table until everything was gone, even the crusts. This made me happy and sad at the same time. Happy that I didn't have to stare at cold cheese all night and sad that Mum wasn't home.

After dinner I went to my room and tried to pretend I was a platypus. I imagined how I had been swimming all day in a brown river, eating lots of bugs and fish and small things that crawled along the riverbed. I imagined how I had stayed underneath the surface of the water all day, except for a few quick moments when I popped my snout up to take a breath and have a look at things. I imagined how proud I would be that no one had seen me, not even people who sat by the river for ages looking really hard. And I imagined that I was in my burrow, and it was small and brown and warm, and I had nothing to worry about and nothing to think about except rivers. I imagined how easy it would be to go to sleep, if you were a platypus.

But I didn't imagine well enough because I couldn't sleep. As soon as I tried my brain started thinking about non-platypus things. Like:

1. Where was Jonas? and

2. Why didn't Jonas tell me he was leaving?

I thought for so long that it got late, and Dad knocked on my door.

"It's late," he said. "Bedtime."

"Dad," I said, because I was getting desperate. "Why wouldn't Jonas tell me he was going to leave?"

"I don't know," Dad said, in a voice that sounded like he was talking from the bottom of a well, and not the space between my room and the hallway. Then he turned off my light and left.

And that was when I started to cry.

I cried so hard that I stopped thinking about why I was crying. I cried for ages to get all the feeling out of me, the way you turn the tap on really hard to get little bits of food out of a clogged-up sink. I cried until my eyes hurt and my nose was blocked and I had to go to the bathroom to get more tissues. And when I was completely empty— of tears and snot and thoughts—I finally fell asleep.

TWENTY-EIGHT

THE NEXT DAY, MRS. ATKINSON GAVE ME homework for Jonas,
so after school I turned left instead of right and knocked
on the door of his house. Peter answered.

"It's spelling worksheets and symmetry," I said, "for
when Jonas comes back." I said "*when* Jonas comes back"
instead of "*if* Jonas comes back" because Peter looked
really sad and I wanted him to feel more hopeful. It
worked—sort of—because he stretched his lips into an
almost-smile and said, "Come in, Cassie. Do you want
some juice?"

I did, and while Peter went to get it I went into Jonas's
room to put the worksheets on his desk. I had never
been in Jonas's room before. The first thing I noticed

was how big it is for just one kid. It's much bigger than my room, and it has more things in it than mine does, like a dartboard and a globe and a laptop. Everything in Jonas's room was tidy—his bed was made (with a shark bedspread and pillowcases) and his clothes were all put away. On Jonas's bookshelf there was a big set of encyclopedias, some other books about science, and a lot of books about sharks. On the wall above Jonas's bed there was a big color poster of the universe, with all the planets and the sun and lots of glittering stars in the background.

None of these things told me anything about Jonas that I didn't already know. I walked over to his desk. His laptop was sitting there with a blank screen, and next to it was a mug of pens and pencils. I sat down and turned on the laptop. After a second the start screen popped up and a little box sat there waiting for a password. Which I didn't have.

I was just about to put the worksheets down and go and find Peter and my juice when I noticed something. On the shelf above Jonas's laptop was a book. And sitting on top of the book was a rock. To anyone else it would have looked like just another river rock. But to me, it was different. To me, it was Jonas's Special Stone.

I took my own Special Stone out of my backpack and compared it to the one on the shelf. They were the same— same flecks, same lumpiness, same smoothness. I felt a little skip of excitement in my stomach. I knew Jonas had left his Special Stone for me (and only me) to find.

I put both of the stones back in my bag. Then I picked up the book that Jonas's Special Stone had been sitting on. It was a copy of *The Adventures of Huckleberry Finn* by Mark Twain. Which is a novel, a story. It's not about facts or science and therefore is not something Jonas is usually interested in. That made me think I might have found a clue, and a little lightbulb of excitement switched on in my brain. I opened the book. There was a bookmark in the middle of chapter eight, which is the chapter where Huck finds Jim on Jackson's Island. The bookmark wasn't a proper bookmark—it was just a piece of paper folded in half. I knew Jonas had a lot of proper bookmarks (most of them shark ones) so the piece of paper in *Huck Finn* was kind of weird. I unfolded it, and written on the inside, in Jonas's handwriting, was one unfinished sentence:

Did you know, the most dangerous part of a
    tiger snake is its . . .

I stared at those three dots for a long time. Then I looked up at the laptop and the little flashing password box. And I started to wonder if maybe Jonas *had* told me why he was leaving. Or at least, he had given me a clue.

I put my hands on the home keys of Jonas's keyboard, and typed:

Venom

The laptop beeped at me, and a red cross flashed up on the screen. I tried again:

Fangs

Another beep. I frowned. I know a lot about tiger snakes, and I know that they are one of the most poisonous snakes in the world. I wondered if Jonas had got his fact wrong. It seemed unlikely. I looked around the room, like I was hoping to see the answer in Jonas's shark bedspread, or his universe poster. My eyes stopped on *Huck Finn*, which I had put on the desk next to the keyboard. And then I thought: What if the answer wasn't a fact at all? What if it was a story? What if it was a story that only Jonas and I knew, because I had told it to him just a few days ago?

I put my pointer fingers back on the F and J keys. And then I typed:

Eyes

The laptop made a happy, chirping sound. I grinned so hard my cheeks hurt—partly because I had typed the right password, but mostly because I knew that Jonas *had* liked my story after all.

Jonas's desktop background filled the screen. It was a photo of a great white shark with its jaws open, coming out of the water. There were little folders and files sitting inside the shark's mouth. I hovered the mouse over them one by one. Recycle Bin. School Stuff. Science Stuff. Animal Stuff. I stopped.

There was a file called The Peacock Detectives.

I opened it. Inside was an address in the city. I took a pencil out of Jonas's mug and copied it down in my Notebook for Noticing. Then I switched off the laptop and turned around just as Peter walked through the door.

"Sorry that took so long," he said. His face was red around the eyes. "I was . . ." Peter was having trouble finishing his sentences. He handed me a big glass of juice.

"It's okay," I said. Because it was. "Thank you."

I took a long sip. It was the most delicious juice I had ever tasted. It was the juice that went with knowing Jonas was my friend, and that he wanted me to find him.

It was the juice of knowing where to begin.

TWENTY-NINE

I KNEW THERE WAS A BUS TO the city at six a.m. because sometimes, after they have finished visiting us, Aunt Sally and
my cousins go home on it. We always drive them to the
bus stop to say goodbye, and it's so early it's still dark, and
Diana and I are drowsy and squashed between our cousins in the back seat. When you're half-awake that early
to meet a bus it's like being in a dream. The world feels
soft and thin, like stretched-out playdough. Like it could
change shape in your hands, or you could push through it
and end up in another world.

I knew you could buy tickets on the bus, too, because
Aunt Sally isn't organized and always forgets to go to the
ticket office the day before, so I took all the pocket money

I had saved out of my money jar and put it together with the fifty dollars Grandpa had given me for Christmas. Altogether it added up to one hundred and fourteen dollars and seventy cents, which I was pretty sure would be enough for one ticket there (for me) and two tickets back (for me and Jonas). I packed the money in my backpack with some water and some cheese sandwiches, my Notebook for Noticing, my photo of Akela, Jonas's birthday present, the two Special Stones, and *Huck Finn* (which I thought would be a good symbol of my mission to find Jonas).

I got up at five a.m., which was easy because I didn't sleep all night. I got dressed and had some Coco-Pops and brushed my teeth and put on my jacket and scarf and beanie and gloves and left the house at five-fifteen. It was dark and cold outside, and I could see frost glittering on the ground in the last bit of moonlight before the sun came up.

To get to the bus stop I had to walk across the bridge and past the hospital and Lee Street and Mum's Flat. In the dark and the cold and the quiet, all those places seemed more alive than usual. Their doors were like mouths and their windows were like eyes following me. They seemed to be breathing. There were no other people out at five fifteen, and I had a thought that if the hospital or Lee Street or Mum's Flat decided they wanted to swallow me up nobody would ever know.

The bus was waiting on the main street, outside the pub. It had its engine on, and it was making a soft rumbling sound. The bus was the only thing in the street with lights on (except for the streetlights) and it looked like one warm glowing star in the middle of a lot of dark space. It reminded me of one of the stars on Jonas's poster, which made me feel a bit braver.

The bus driver was reading a newspaper and eating an apple in the front seat.

"Morning," she said, except it sounded more like "ornin" because her mouth was full of Red Delicious. "Ot a icket?"

I shook my head and took a twenty dollar bill and four dollars and forty in change out of my bag. The bus driver swallowed.

"On your own, love?"

I nodded. "I'm going to visit my aunt," I said, which was almost the truth because I had written Aunt Sally's phone number in my Notebook for Noticing in case I got into trouble. The bus driver had one eyebrow raised like she didn't quite believe me, so I added, "She's meeting me at the station." This was in no way The Truth, but I decided it was a Necessary Lie because Jonas was counting on me.

The bus driver took my money and gave me a ticket.

"Have a seat," she said.

I was the first person on the bus. It was warm, and the light was soft. I sat at the back and huddled up next to the window in my jacket to watch everyone else get on. I felt like I was staking them out, since I was kind of invisible in the almost-dark. It was nice to feel like a detective again.

The first person to get on the bus after me was an old woman. She had a big fluffy coat and a nice handbag and she was wearing lipstick. Next, a man got on by himself and chatted for a while to the bus driver about his kids and football, so I deduced he must ride the bus a lot. Then a man and a woman got on, and they looked like tourists because they had shopping bags from the Bloomsbury Information Center and backpacks. They sat down together and fell asleep on each other's heads and shoulders before the bus even left. Seeing them like that made me wish I had someone's head and shoulder to fall asleep on, too.

We were just about to leave (I could tell because the bus driver turned the engine up and the lights down) when a girl ran onto the bus. She was puffing and she didn't have a ticket, which the bus driver was a bit cross about because it meant she had to take money and give out change when it was already six o'clock. The girl was wearing jeans and a sweater—she didn't have a beanie or gloves or a coat—and her backpack was stuffed so full that the zipper couldn't zip up properly.

Finally, the bus driver closed the door and sat in the driver's seat. The girl turned around. The bus clock clicked over to 6:03 and the light hit the girl's face just enough for me to see who she was. And seeing who she was made me huddle deeper into my jacket.

Because the girl was Rhea Grimm.

Ever since Rhea Grimm had come back from being suspended, I had tried my best not to cross paths with her. I had faked a headache so I didn't have to go to the oval for PE, and I told Mrs. Atkinson I couldn't do the lunch orders because I wanted to improve my math skills. But the-bus-at-six-a.m. was not a place I had expected to cross paths with Rhea Grimm.

She wanted to sit at the back of the bus—I could tell by the way she was scanning the seats. But she also wanted to sit alone, so she took the seat across the aisle from me, next to the window. I realized with some despair that I would have to stay bundled up against my own window for the rest of the trip if I didn't want Rhea Grimm to see me. Which I really didn't. Especially since this time I had no Jonas with balloons full of peanut butter and tomato sauce to rescue me.

We finally started to leave just as the clock ticked over to 6:05. The bus was so big that it felt like I was on a ship pulling away from the shore. The bus took a long time to turn, and while it did I silently said goodbye to all the things I knew. The newsagent, the supermarket, the gas station. And then we were driving fast and straight, right out of town. It was still dark enough to see stars, and from my low-down huddled position looking up and out of the big bus window it felt like we were driving through space.

I stared out the window until 7:24 and then I risked emerging a little bit from my hiding place. I couldn't see Rhea Grimm's face—she was either looking out her window or sleeping. Everyone else on the bus seemed to be asleep, too—except for the old lady, who was doing a crossword (a normal one, not a cryptic one). If I looked down the aisle I could see out the front window, which was as big as a movie screen. It was slowly becoming day-time but the light was still making everything fuzzy at the edges. It was like the world had fallen apart during the night and was now slowly putting itself back together. We went past a lot of fuzzy trees, and here and there a fuzzy house, a fuzzy dog, a fuzzy paddock of sleeping-upright cows.

I realized that if I had been at home now I would have been waking up to eat breakfast. And in forty-five min-utes I would be walking to school with Diana. Somewhere between now and then Dad and Diana would realize I was missing. I tried not to think about what their faces would look like when they found me not there. I had left a note on my pillow that said:

Gone to find Jonas. DON'T WORRY!!

I really hoped writing *DON'T WORRY!!* like that (in capitals with two exclamation marks) would make the words more powerful, so that Dad and Diana really wouldn't worry. But I had a feeling words wouldn't be enough—especially words written by someone who is only eleven-turning-twelve on a piece of paper torn out of the back of a notebook.

I stopped imagining Dad and Diana reading my note and imagined finding Jonas instead. In my imagination he was really happy to see me, and when I said, "You should come home now," he said, "Okay." And then we ate city ice cream (which is completely different from country ice cream and more delicious) and then we came home.

Even though I knew finding Jonas wouldn't be so easy, imagining it like that made me feel better, and I fell asleep against the big bus window.

When I woke up it was definitely daytime. All the blurry edges had smoothed themselves out like freshly ironed clothes and everything was clear and bright. We were driving fast past big green paddocks and small hills. The clock said 9:02, which meant it was almost time for me to change from the bus to the train.

I looked over at Rhea Grimm. She was still facing the window. I picked up my bag and my jacket and got ready to get off the bus before she did. I knew exactly what to do and where to go, because Aunt Sally always complains (in lots of detail) about how annoying it is to change from the bus to the train. In case you ever need to know, changing from the bus to the train goes like this:

1. You get off the bus and go down under the bridge and up the other side onto Platform 1.
2. You look for the train.
3. You look at your ticket to see which car you are in. If your ticket says "unreserved" it means you are in the last car, and you can sit in any seat you want.
4. You get on the train. (If you are trying to avoid someone else who is also going to be getting on the train you sit next to a window and huddle yourself up against it.)

Because I had practiced these steps over and over in my head the night before (except for the bit about avoiding someone) I thought I was really ready to change from the bus to the train. I got off the bus faster than anyone else, and ran-walked down the hill and under the bridge. But when I came up the other side there was no train on the platform.

Panic started rising in my stomach like a shaken-up can of soft drink. I knew Rhea Grimm was somewhere under the bridge behind me, and there was no one to ask for help. I started to wish more than anything that I had someone with me, like Diana or Jonas, or even Simon. I looked up and down the platform, just in case the train was still coming down the tracks. It wasn't. But as I was looking left I noticed a sign. And the sign said:

PLATFORM 2

I turned around. Behind me was another sign, and it said:

PLATFORM 1

And behind that sign was the train.

I quickly got in the last car and sighed with relief. I watched everybody else as they walked along Platform 1. Rhea Grimm was last. The train was starting to whistle like it was getting ready to leave, but Rhea Grimm still wasn't on it. She was standing on the platform looking down at her ticket, and then up at the train, and then down at her ticket again. For a second I almost felt sorry for her, but then I remembered how she had called my dad crazy and a loser, and how much she had wanted to make me sad. So instead of feeling sorry I closed my eyes for a second and breathed and didn't-think and tried to feel nothing.

At the last minute a man in an orange vest came over

and looked at Rhea Grimm's ticket. He pointed to the unreserved car. I've never seen Rhea Grimm look at someone nicely. Ever. Not even her friends. But when she looked at the man with the orange vest her eyes were so grateful. Really grateful, not in that twisted, slimy way that she is usually grateful, like when she makes someone give her their lunch or their pocket money. I wondered if it was really Rhea Grimm getting on the train with me, or if she had a secret twin sister who was actually nice.

Then another whistle blew, and Rhea Grimm got into the unreserved car, and the train started to chug away from the station with a steady, determined sound.

After a while the scenery started to change. There weren't so many green paddocks—most of them were brown. And instead of farmhouses there were gas stations and truck stops. The sky turned slowly from blue to gray, like it was hoping nobody would notice. Then I saw a big stone building that had barbed wire around it and graffiti on the sides. And that was when I knew we were in The City.

I didn't feel like I was riding in a spaceship anymore. Instead, I had the feeling that I was inside a snake, sliding quietly and steadily along the tracks. I wondered if Jonas had felt the same feeling. I wondered if Rhea Grimm felt it now, too.

THIRTY

THESE ARE MY FOUR BEST MEMORIES OF The City:

1. Driving in the car with Mum and Dad and Diana, and playing I-Spy.
2. Staying at Aunt Sally's house, which has a big backyard and a cage full of parakeets.
3. Playing Monopoly and eating lasagna and ice cream.
4. Going to a really big shopping center and sitting on Santa's knee and telling him that for Christmas I wanted three books and a bike.

In these memories The City is fun, chirpy, and full of presents. But the place that I was sliding through in the train was smoky and huge and confusing. There were big signs for things I had never heard of, like Housing Estates and Gentlemen's Clubs and Bargain Warehouses. There were broken windows and fences, and lots of houses and parks with grass that wasn't cut. And there were so many people walking and driving and running and bike riding but none of them stopped to say hello to anyone else. Nobody seemed to pause for even a second to say, "Did you see the football last night?" or "Nice day!" or "How's Liz?" I started to wonder—for the first time since I had made my plan to find Jonas—if this was a good idea after all.

When the train stopped I wasn't sure I wanted to get off it. The people walking along the platform looked like they knew exactly where they were going. They looked like they all had plans, and knew how to carry them out.

I had written down my plan in my notebook. It looked like this:

Step One: Get off the train.

Step Two: Find an Information Booth.

Step Three: Find out how to get to the address I had found on Jonas's laptop.

Step Four: Go there.

Step Five: Find Jonas.

Step Six: Make him come home.

On the bus I was sure of my plan. On the train I was a little less sure. And now that I was in The City I wasn't sure at all. Now my plan was getting pecked apart by questions, the way a head of lettuce gets pecked apart by chickens. What if I couldn't find an Information Booth? What if Jonas wasn't at the address I had written down? And (this was the question that pecked the hardest) even if I found Jonas, what if he refused to come home?

I wished more than anything that I had somebody to ask these questions. But there was only me. I suddenly felt more alone than I ever had in my whole life.

I sat in my seat for so long that I was the last person left on the train. Or at least, I thought I was the last person. But then I heard someone crying softly behind me. I turned around. The person crying had brown hair in a ponytail and lots of jangling bracelets. The person crying was Rhea Grimm.

I wondered if I should make a break for it while she was distracted. I could get off the train and quickly walk to the end of the platform without looking back. But when I picked up my backpack I remembered how Grandpa had given it to me. I thought about how Grandpa would feel if he saw me walking away from someone who was crying—even a usually-very-mean someone. I thought about how I had Aunt Sally's phone number in my notebook, and if something really bad happened (like if Rhea Grimm beat me up and stole all my money) I could ask someone to call her. And these two thoughts together made me stand up and turn around and reveal myself to Rhea Grimm.

She didn't notice me at first because her eyes were all teary. When she finally wiped her eyes and saw me, I almost ran away, because that is what I usually do when Rhea Grimm sees me. But I thought about Grandpa and stood my ground. Rhea Grimm sniffed. Hard.

"Andersen," she said. There was much less meanness in her voice than usual. "What are you doing here?"

"Looking for Jonas," I said, because right then I couldn't think of anything better to say than The Truth. "Are you okay?"

Rhea Grimm rubbed her eyes with her knuckles and said—with a little more meanness this time—"I'm fine. Stop staring at me."

"All right," I said, and I started to turn around. Rhea Grimm had sniffed back all her tears, so at least I wasn't walking away from someone who was crying.

I was halfway to the door when Rhea Grimm said, "Cassie. Wait."

That was the first time Rhea Grimm had ever called me Cassie. I was so surprised that I turned back. Then Rhea Grimm did something else she had never done before. She smiled at me. It was a weak, watery smile, but it was real. It was a smile that said, "Don't leave me here." And something inside me sagged with relief, because I really didn't want to be alone in the train station either.

For a minute nothing happened. Then a man with a big plastic bag walked past us and picked up some rubbish.

"Maybe we should get off," I said, and Rhea Grimm nodded. We got our backpacks and stepped out the door and onto the platform. It was much colder outside the train, and sounds that had been muffled before were now very loud and clear. Rhea Grimm breathed out a long sigh, and I knew how she felt. And how she felt was that getting off that train was a lot like climbing to the top of a mountain.

After we had stood on the platform for a while—feeling puffed-out from getting off the train and cold—Rhea Grimm said, "I'm starving." I realized I was, too, and so we followed our stomachs through the station to a small café. Rhea Grimm had some money, and she bought us both hot chocolates and toasted cheese sandwiches (I was still too scared of Rhea Grimm to tell her that I was sick of toasted cheese). The woman at the counter smiled at us and asked if we were sisters.

I was about to say no, but Rhea Grimm was faster than me. "Yes," she said.

When we sat down she whispered, "Just pretend. It's less suspicious."

My hot chocolate was really hot and tasted more like milk than chocolate. I burned my tongue on the first sip, and after that I couldn't taste anything (which I was upset about because Rhea Grimm was eating her toasted cheese sandwich so fast it must have been the most delicious toasted cheese sandwich ever). When she was finished she wiped her mouth with a napkin and put her elbows on the table and stared at me. I took a bite of my sandwich and a really stringy piece of melted cheese got stuck between the bread and my mouth. It kept getting longer and longer and wouldn't break. Having someone like Rhea Grimm stare at you while you have a piece of cheese hanging from your teeth is one of the most uncomfortable things in the world. The longer the cheese got the more I expected Rhea Grimm to say something mean like "Hey, Booger Lips" or "Nice one, Cheese Face." But she didn't say anything. Until the cheese finally broke and I quickly piled it all into my mouth and chewed and swallowed. Then Rhea Grimm said, "Where's Jonas?"

I showed her the address in my notebook and told her about my plan to find an Information Booth. She didn't look very interested, so I was surprised when she said, "Let's go, then."

I put the rest of my sandwich on its plate and pushed it toward the salt and pepper shakers. I was too surprised (and tongue-burnt) to eat anymore.

"What?" I said.

"I'll come with you," Rhea Grimm said, picking up my sandwich.

"To find Jonas?"

"Yeah." She took a bite.

"Frog Eyes?"

"Yes." She was chewing, so it sounded more like "es."

"The boy who threw tomato sauce and peanut butter balloons at you?"

"I know who Jonas is."

I wondered for a moment if Rhea Grimm wanted to find Jonas so she could get back at him for the balloon incident. I couldn't ask her, though, because if that was her plan she would probably just lie. I had to catch her off guard.

"Why were you on the train?" I asked.

Rhea Grimm sort of curled up into herself, which is pretty hard to do when you're sitting in a train station café, but she managed it. "It's personal," she said.

I nodded. I knew about Personal. Personal was what Diana wrote in the diary under her mattress. Personal was Mum's list in her bedside drawer. Personal was Dad going to The Clinic. I was suspicious of Personal, but I was also worried about finding Jonas in The City on my own. So I said, "All right, you can come," and I decided to keep an eye on her.

We found an Information Booth. It had streaky windows and a woman inside. I showed the woman—who was very round with light brown hair and bright red lipstick—the address in my Notebook for Noticing.

She looked at us a little strangely at first, but then Rhea Grimm held my hand in a sisterly sort of way, and the woman smiled.

"That's not too far," she said. "You can take a tram." She told us which number and we paid for our tickets and then she pointed to the Exit. It was a big wide opening, like something enormous had taken a large bite.

Suddenly the station felt very familiar compared to the big city outside. The tracks felt like old friends, the platform felt like the Bloomsbury main street, the café felt like Mum's kitchen. But we were on a mission. I looked at Rhea Grimm, and we started walking.

THIRTY-ONE

THE DEPARTMENT OF HUMAN SERVICES WAS A big gray building on the corner of a small gray street. The tram dropped us off right outside, and for a minute Rhea Grimm and I stood on the footpath and stared up at the rows of dark windows. I thought about how long ago the six-a.m. bus felt. My plan only had two steps left: Step Five: Find Jonas, and Step Six: Make him come home.

The Department of Human Services had automatic sliding doors, and inside them was a big room with waiting chairs and tables and a Help Desk with a man behind it. I asked the man how to get to Adoption and Permanent Care.

"Fifth floor," he said, and leaned across his desk. He

was looking at us like we were some kind of rare species of animal. "Where's your mum?"

"Outside," Rhea Grimm said. She grabbed my hand and pulled me toward the elevator. "She's just having a cigarette." Before the man could ask us any more questions we were in the elevator and going up.

On the fifth floor there was a smaller room with chairs and tables covered in brochures and magazines. There was another desk, too, except the sign above this one said Documents and Records. I opened my Notebook for Noticing to double-check. At the bottom of the page, underneath the address, I had written:

Department of Human Services

Adoption and Permanent Care

Applying for Documents and Records

And I knew we were in the right place.

The lady at this desk had brown hair with bits of gray in it, and glasses. She didn't smile at us. Her name tag said "Lynda."

"Hello, Lynda," I said, because Mum says it's polite to use people's names if you know them. Then I gave Lynda my description of Jonas, which I had been practicing in my head for the whole tram ride.

It went like this: "We are looking for a boy. His name is Jonas Alan Mallory and he just turned twelve years old. He is a bit taller than me and he has brown hair. He wears glasses even though he doesn't really need to, because he thinks they make him look like Stephen Hawking, who is his favorite scientist. He is very smart for his age. He is especially good at science and math, and he can read and write at a Year Seven level. His favorite animals are sharks, and he knows lots of interesting facts. Have you seen him?"

Lynda looked at me without saying anything (or smiling) for a long time. Then she said, "Where are your parents?"

"Mum's outside," Rhea Grimm said. "She just *had* to have a smoke." Rhea Grimm gave Lynda the same look my mum gives people when she is complaining about Simon digging up the garden. It's a grown-up look that means I'm really not happy about this situation, but what can I do? I thought Rhea Grimm did a pretty good job of this look, but I don't think Lynda agreed. She went on frowning, and then she turned and yelled into a small room behind the desk: "Sam!"

Another woman appeared. She had a pink jacket and soft brown hair that was almost red. She wasn't wearing a name tag but I knew her name was Sam, because Lynda had just yelled it.

"Hello, Sam," I said, and then I repeated my description of Jonas. By the time I got to the end—the bit about the sharks and Jonas knowing lots of facts—my voice was shaking. I was sure that when I finished Sam and Lynda would tell us to leave, or call the police or our parents, or all of the above. We would never find Jonas, and he would never know that I had figured out his clue.

But then Sam said, "Interesting facts? Like, did you know the bullfrog is the only animal that never sleeps?"

"Yes!" I said. I was so happy to hear one of Jonas's facts coming out of Sam's mouth that I wanted to jump over the desk and hug her. But I didn't. Instead I said, "Is he here?"

"He was here," Sam said. When she said the word "was" my stomach started to get heavy. "Was" is a past-tense word. It means had been, but isn't anymore. "He came in yesterday morning. He said he was doing a school project. Are you girls from the same class?"

"Yes," I said, in a voice like a sigh. Yesterday was so long ago.

"Did you tell him anything?" Rhea Grimm asked.

"Not really," Sam said. "He wanted names and addresses. We're not allowed to give out information like that."

"Did he say anything before he left?" I asked.

"No," Sam said, "but he had a terrible bloody nose."

My insides felt like an elastic band that had been pulled really tight and then suddenly snapped back. Just a few minutes ago on the tram I had been full of hope. Now I was full of nothing.

"I'm sorry I can't be more helpful, girls," Sam said.

"It's okay," Rhea Grimm said. "We have to go back to school now."

And then we were in the elevator, and then we were on the ground floor, and then we were on the footpath again. And when we got there I didn't know what to do, because I had no Jonas. And no plan.

We sat on a bench at the tram stop. I tried my hardest to think like Jonas. I imagined that it was Jonas sitting on this hard metal tram-stop bench staring at his hands, and not me. I imagined that it was Jonas's watch on my wrist, and not mine (this was easy, since Jonas and I had synchronized our watches for the stakeout, so I knew they were telling exactly the same time). Then I tried to understand what it would have felt like for Jonas to come to the big gray Department of Human Services building all by himself. I tried to understand what it would have felt like for him to go up to the fifth floor, looking for his real parents, and then to hear Sam say, "I'm sorry I can't be more helpful." I tried to understand what he must have been thinking, with his head tilted back to keep his nose from bleeding all over Adoption and Permanent Care. And I tried to figure out where he would have gone next.

The more I thought, the more figuring it out seemed impossible. I couldn't feel Jonas's feelings like he could. I felt like a bad detective and a bad storyteller. A bad detective because I couldn't follow clues properly, and a bad storyteller because I didn't understand Jonas's story well enough to know what should happen next.

While I was sitting there feeling sad about Jonas and sorry for myself, Rhea Grimm was walking up and down the tram platform. After a few minutes she said, "Why does Jonas like sharks so much?"

"Huh?"

"I mean, they're not very nice animals. They just swim around all day killing things. They've got horrible teeth and gross eyes. I don't get it."

I tried to remember all the facts Jonas had told me about sharks. They can swim twenty-four kilometers an hour. They can smell blood from five kilometers away. They have three hundred teeth. They can jump completely out of the water to catch their food.

These were all interesting facts, but I didn't think any of them was the reason sharks were Jonas's favorite animal.

Then I remembered something else Jonas had told me about sharks. It was lunchtime, and we were sitting on (Jonas) and near (me) The Snake Stairs. It was one of the days after Grandpa went to hospital when we were only telling sad stories and disturbing-but-interesting facts. Jonas had been quiet all day, and we were chewing and not talking. Then suddenly Jonas swallowed and yelled across the path at me—

"Did you know if a shark stops swimming it will die?"

"How do they sleep, then?" I yelled back.

"Even when they're sleeping," Jonas said. "Even then, they have to keep swimming."

"Or what?"

"Or they drown. They just sink to the bottom. And they drown."

I pictured sharks falling to the bottom of the ocean like helium balloons that had run out of helium.

"They must get really tired," I yelled.

"Yeah," Jonas yelled back. "But they keep on going. Because they really, really want to stay alive."

Jonas didn't look at me when he said that last part. He was staring into the bushes and his eyes had a funny look, like they had turned around and were staring into himself instead of out into the world. And even though what Jonas had said about sharks was a fact, the way he said it made it feel like it was a story.

I jumped up from the cold tram-stop bench. "I know where he's gone!" I cried.

"Huh?" Rhea Grimm said.

I grabbed her hand. There was a tram coming, and we needed to get on it. "Come on," I said, and suddenly I was full of hope again.

THIRTY-TWO

JONAS WAS SITTING ON ONE OF THOSE big carpeted blocks in The Fish Bowl. It's called The Fish Bowl because it's the part of the aquarium that has glass walls and a glass ceiling and behind the glass are fish. The water was making wavy shadows across his face, and when a really big fish swam over the top, it was hard to see that it was really Jonas sitting there. His face was colored-in by fish shadows.

I sat down on one side of Jonas and Rhea Grimm sat down on the other. This was part of my plan, so if Jonas tried to run away it would be easier to stop him. When Jonas saw Rhea Grimm, his eyes widened for a second in surprise. Then he went back to staring at the stingrays and the nurse sharks and the sea turtles.

"This is for you," I said, and I put his birthday present on the bit of block between us. It was a Peacock Detective badge with his name on it and a picture of a peacock feather. There was a safety pin attached to the back. Jonas looked at it, but he didn't pick it up.

"Thanks," he said. Then there was silence except for the aquarium soundtrack that isn't quite music but isn't quite whale sounds, either. Then Jonas said, "I knew you'd find me."

I turned to look at him. A grouper swam behind his head. "How did you know?"

Jonas smiled the tiniest smile. So tiny that if I had blinked at that second I would have missed it. "Because you're a Peacock Detective."

The aquarium soundtrack sounded like dolphins singing. "Let's go home," I said.

A stingray flew over our heads, like a pterodactyl. Jonas's face went dark.

"Home," he said, except it sounded like he was saying a nonsense word. A word like *flibbertygizzit* or *babbleflap*. A word with no meaning.

"Mississippi Street, Bloomsbury," I said, thinking maybe I could get his attention with specific details. "Number twenty-four."

Jonas stared at a big school of little fish.

"Left from school, and past the church. Around the corner," I tried.

Jonas still said nothing. An eel went past like a long piece of tree bark.

"The brick house with the really big front yard. There are always weeds in the grass even though Peter picks them out every Saturday. And on the veranda there's a wind chime that Irene bought in China. It's shaped like a fish and it makes a noise that you think sounds like fresh air, if fresh air had a sound."

The grouper again. A nurse shark. Another grouper. I was getting desperate. I wanted to shake Jonas, or slap him the way they do in books when people are being unreasonable. "Your mum and dad live there!" I cried finally, in a voice that was too loud for The Fish Bowl.

"They're not my mum and dad," Jonas said, which is what I knew he was going to say, but which I didn't have an answer for. I closed my mouth and sat in quiet, frustrated silence.

"Why not?" said Rhea Grimm.

I was surprised when she spoke. Jonas was surprised, too—I could tell because for the first time he turned his face away from the fish.

"Don't they look after you?" Rhea Grimm said.

Jonas stared at Rhea Grimm, and Rhea Grimm stared back. For a long time Jonas didn't answer, and there was only the sound of dolphins mixed with clarinet. Then he said, "Yeah. They look after me."

"Do they cook you dinner?"

"Yeah."

"Do they buy you school clothes and books and throw you birthday parties?"

"Yeah."

Rhea Grimm crossed her arms. "They're your parents, then. Parents do all that stuff."

"They're not my real parents, though. You know. Scientifically."

I was staring at a starfish that had suctioned itself to the glass. Then I remembered something Mum had said: *Just because a story's not true doesn't mean it's not good.*

I turned to Jonas. "Maybe they're not your parents in a fact-way," I said. "But they are your parents in another way. In the way of buying you a laptop, and all those encyclopedias. And in the way of loving you."

"But it's a lie," Jonas said, and his voice shook. He turned back to the fish, and I could see tears sitting in his eyes.

"No," I said. "It's a Metaphor."

We all sat still for a long time then, watching the fish. The aquarium soundtrack sounded like waves crashing, with violins. One of the nurse sharks was swimming over our heads, back and forth, never stopping. I counted its belly above me ten times. After the tenth time Jonas picked up his birthday present, and stood up.

"Come on," he said. "We can still get the last train."

On the way back to the station Jonas pinned his Peacock Detective badge to his shirt.

"You don't have to wear it," I said. "You can just keep it in your bag, if you want."

"I want to wear it," Jonas said. Which made me feel happy all the way down to my toes.

Rhea Grimm was really quiet. She'd been quiet since her speech in the Fish Bowl. And when we were standing at the ticket counter holding hands and pretending to be brother and sisters, she let go.

Jonas was standing at the counter with his money. The ticket man had a long thin face and wrinkles in his forehead. He was watching us carefully.

"Come on," I whispered, with my teeth clenched so the ticket man wouldn't hear me. "We all have to go together."

Rhea Grimm's face crumpled like it was a supermarket receipt about to be thrown in the bin. Then she turned around and ran, faster than I've ever seen anyone run before. She ran right across the station and out the big gaping hole of the Exit. And into the almost-dark street.

When I first started writing this story I thought that Rhea Grimm was A Minor Character. A Minor Character is someone who has a small part in a story. Minor

Characters are only really useful because of their connections to Main Characters (like Tom Golding, because he is connected to Diana) or because they do things that keep the story going (like the bus driver, because she drove the bus so I could get to the city to find Jonas). But while I was standing there watching Rhea Grimm's shoes disappear out of the train station I thought about all the things she had done. I thought about how she had been crying on the train, and how she had come with me to the Department of Human Services building, and how she had asked me about sharks. And I knew I wouldn't have been able to find Jonas without her. And suddenly I realized Rhea wasn't A Minor Character after all—in my story, she was A Main Character.

Jonas was standing at the ticket counter with his eyes wide and his mouth open. The ticket man had pushed his lips together like he didn't believe we were brother and sisters at all and was about to call someone and tell on us. I grabbed Jonas and his money and pulled him toward the Exit.

Out on the street we looked left and right, and I saw Rhea's messy ponytail darting past a café. We ran after her. She was really fast—if someone had been giving out ribbons for running through the city, Rhea would have got the blue one. She ran past a bank and around a corner. Jonas and I dodged a blind woman with a dog, and then almost ran into two men in suits. They yelled at us to

"Watch it!" and I wanted to say sorry but we were losing Rhea and had no time. At the next intersection, I wished really hard for the red light so Rhea would have to stop and we could catch her. But the light stayed green and she escaped across the road. Jonas was puffing. I yelled at him to hurry up and then I almost ran into a car that was parked half on the footpath.

Up ahead was a big park—I could see the tops of bushy city trees and painted pavilions for sitting and reading and having picnics in. Rhea ran into the park and for a moment I thought we had lost her. We ran through the trees, and it felt like maybe we would have to give up and go home without her. Which yesterday I would not have minded at all, but today I really, really did.

And then we saw her. She was sitting on the grass, slumped against the trunk of an enormous city tree. She looked like she never wanted to get up again.

Jonas and I were breathing so hard we had to wait a minute before we could say anything. And even when we had our breath back we didn't know what to say. Rhea was staring at her knees. I sat down next to her and stared at my knees, too. Jonas did the same, but on the other side of Rhea (in case she tried to run away again). And then we were all sitting in the city park, so far away from everything we knew, staring and not-talking.

We stayed like that until it was too dark to see our knees anymore. Then I stood up, and then Jonas stood up, and then Rhea did, too. We walked back to the station and Jonas paid for our tickets and we got on the train.

Rhea didn't tell us why she had run away, and Jonas and I didn't ask her. We fell asleep on each other's heads and shoulders, and when we had to change to the bus it felt like we were sleepwalking down the platform.

When we got back to Bloomsbury it was very dark and very late. We walked home together until just before the hospital, and then Rhea turned down a dark street. She waved goodbye without speaking. I wondered if she was thinking about her Personal thing. While Jonas and I were crossing the bridge he told me about how he had slept in the train station last night, and about how he had felt when he got to the Department of Human Services building.

"I thought if I went all the way there they would have to take me to my real parents," he said. "But they wouldn't even tell me their names. Everything just felt black, after that. Like a universe with no stars."

Before Jonas turned left and went home I took his Special Stone out of my backpack and gave it to him. Then I asked him the question I had wanted to ask him for two days.

"Why didn't you tell me you were leaving?"

For a moment there was only the cold quiet of winter night. Then Jonas said, "Because I knew you'd tell me a story that would make me stay. And I had to go."

"Why did you leave the Special Stone, then?"

Jonas smiled. "Because I also knew you would find me if things didn't work out."

I nodded. "I knew I would, too," I said, because—deep down—I had.

We said goodbye and I walked the rest of the way home by myself, thinking how weird it was for someone to want to run away and be found at the same time.

When I got home I noticed four things:

1. All the lights were on even though it was almost midnight.
2. Diana and Simon were inside.
3. Mum and Dad were sitting on the couch holding hands, and
4. My mum is really, really beautiful.

When I walked in and saw them all like that my stomach twisted into a big knot of guilt and fear and love and hunger and tiredness. For a moment nobody did anything—we all just stared at each other. Then Dad started crying. Mum jumped up and hugged me so hard I thought my eyeballs were going to squeeze out of their sockets. Simon licked me on every bit of bare skin he could find. And Diana said, "Everyone thought you were dead, you idiot," which in fifteen-year-old language means "I missed you."

All the way home I had prepared myself for being in

big trouble. I explained to Mum and Dad that I couldn't tell them about Jonas because his clue was just for me (cross my heart), and then I said sorry for the note I had left (the one that said *DON'T WORRY!!* in capital letters).

But I wasn't in trouble. Everyone was too busy being happy I was home to think of a way to punish me. Mum made hot chocolate (with cocoa powder and milk and sugar and marshmallows, and just the right amount of hot) and Dad said I could stay up until one thirty. Diana stayed inside all night on a mattress on my floor. She talked until I fell asleep about how everyone had been looking for me all day, and about Buddhism, and about how Year Nine was harder than she thought it would be. She didn't talk about Tom Golding, but I could tell from her pauses (because even though we are three years apart she is still my sister) that she wanted to.

While I was listening to her I thought about Jonas, and Rhea. I wondered if they had had hot chocolate, too. I wondered if their parents had cried and hugged them until their eyeballs hurt. I knew Jonas's would have. I wasn't so sure about Rhea's.

THIRTY-THREE

DAD SAID I DIDN'T HAVE TO GO to school this morning because I had been missing and I had stayed up so late, but I really wanted to see Jonas and Rhea. Before I left, Dad gave me a giant hug—the kind of hug he used to give before Grandpa got sick and Mum moved out—and for a minute I thought he wasn't going to let me go. But then he did, and he watched Diana and me until we were all the way to the end of the street. We turned the corner and couldn't see him anymore, but I knew he was still there.

Jonas was waiting for me at the school gate.

"I stayed up until one forty-five!" I said, as soon as I was close enough for him to hear me. "And Mum made hot chocolate."

"Mum made French toast," Jonas said. "And I went on the internet for two hours. Did you know vultures help prevent diseases from spreading?"

It was good to hear Jonas talking about interesting facts again, and to hear him call his mum Mum, instead of Irene. He said his mum and dad had tried to be mad at him for sleeping alone in a train station—which I guess was pretty dangerous—but it didn't really work since they couldn't stop smiling and hugging him. We went to class and I could tell Mrs. Atkinson was glad to see us because she didn't give us catch-up spelling worksheets for being absent. We did story-writing (I wrote about an explorer who gets lost in a train station) and science (Jonas answered all Mrs. Atkinson's questions about bacteria) and then at little recess we went looking for Rhea.

To find her we had to cross the handball courts. After going to The City and back, crossing the handball courts wasn't as scary as it used to be. I felt more twelve than eleven knowing I had caught a bus and a train by myself. It was also nice to be going to visit someone in secondary school who wasn't my sister or my dad. As we walked past the lockers I felt less like a small animal in danger of being eaten and more like a medium-size animal on her way to meet a friend.

We found Rhea on the basketball courts. She was playing Around the World with her friends—the same friends

Jonas had thrown peanut butter and tomato sauce at. She was getting lots of shots in, and she was laughing. She looked like a girl who had never even thought about running away, let alone actually done it.

"She looks all right," Jonas said, in a secondary school whisper. "Maybe we should leave her alone." Jonas hadn't spent as much time with Rhea as I had. He hadn't seen her smile at the conductor on the platform, or cry on the train, so he was still scared of her.

"Let's just say hi," I said. "Come on."

I should have known something wasn't right when Rhea saw us and stopped laughing. One of her friends grabbed the basketball and the friendly bouncing and hoop-swooshing sounds stopped. Rhea was staring at us. Her friends were staring at us. There was a horrible silence, the kind of silence that happens in a forest when a large predator is about to attack.

I tried smiling but my smile felt like very weak cordial. "Hi," I said, and my voice sounded like the voice of a ghost—thin, and not very believable. I could feel Jonas poking the back of my ankle with his shoe. I knew he was trying to tell me it was time to go, but I also knew it was too late.

"What do you want, Andersen?" One of the girls who wasn't Rhea said, in a voice like an unpinned safety pin.

"I just . . ." I started, but stopped when I saw Rhea's

face. I was going to ask if she was okay, and if she had been allowed to stay up late, and if she wanted to come with me and Jonas to look for the peacocks after school. But then I saw the way she was looking at me. It was the same way Simon looks at his poo when he can't find enough dirt to cover it up with. It was an embarrassed look. An ashamed look. Except instead of being embarrassed by uncovered poo, Rhea was embarrassed by me.

I felt my face go red from my neck up to my hair. I turned around and grabbed Jonas and we started running. We didn't stop until we were on the other side of the handball courts, and then we sat under the monkey bars and looked at each other. I could tell Jonas was thinking I told you so, except he was too much my friend to say it.

I looked down at my feet. I was thinking about the Rhea from yesterday—the Rhea who had pretended to be my sister and had bought me lunch. The Rhea who had sat next to me on a tram all the way across The City. The Rhea who had called me Cassie. And I was thinking how weird it was for one person to be two people—one who is nice and who smiles and wants to hold hands in train stations, and one who is mean and ashamed and wants to make the people who care about them feel like dog poo.

PART THREE

Spring & Summer

THIRTY-FOUR

FOR A WHILE EVERYTHING WENT ALONG AS normal, except for a few things. For example: Simon taking all of Dad's shoes and burying them in the backyard (I think he was angry at Dad for never walking him), and Diana sneaking into the house in the middle of the night to watch TV and charge her phone. She thinks no one notices, but I do, because I'm a Peacock Detective and a writer, and I'm good at noticing details.

I started reading books again. In August and September I read *Gulliver's Travels*, *The Hobbit*, and *The Lord of the Flies* (which Dad was teaching for Year Eight English). I've been writing more stories, too. I give them to Mrs. Atkinson to read, and she says they are some of my best stories yet. And I started a new To-Do List. It looks like this:

1. Find the peacocks, who were still at large.
2. Find out what Buddhism is.
3. Be friends with Rhea.

In October it was my birthday, which means I'm not eleven-turning-twelve anymore. I'm completely twelve. I had three birthday parties this year: one with Dad (we ordered pizza and watched *Jurassic Park*, which is an old movie, but still a good movie), one with Mum and Roger (Mum made a Castle Cake, and it was the best and most complicated cake she has ever made), and one with Diana and Jonas (we went out for pancakes and blue heaven spiders, which would have been the best birthday party of them all, except that Tom Golding was there and he kept looking at Diana in a weird way, and she kept not-looking at him in a weird way, which left Jonas and me sitting in an awkward way).

Mum is still living at The Flat, and Dad is still at home. Diana is talking to Dad less and less, and not-being at home more and more (which was why she didn't join the pizza–*Jurassic Park* party). But—maybe because I'm twelve now, or maybe because I had been missing, or maybe both—Diana and I are talking to each other again. Sometimes I visit her in her tent, and sometimes she comes and lies on my floor before I go to sleep. In October Diana told me—carefully and quietly, like her words were made of glass and might break—that the doctors said Grandpa only has a few months left. I think Diana was afraid that when she said this I would get mad and stomp off, like I did last time. But I didn't. And now we talk about Grandpa all the time. Not about Grandpa being sick, just about Grandpa being Grandpa. We talk about how much he loves crosswords, and how I like to sit next to him in church, and how he always talks about his garden. And instead of making me feel upset and scared, talking about Grandpa this way makes me feel sort of light, like I have been carrying around a really heavy backpack but now I can finally take it off.

October also means spring. Spring in Bloomsbury sounds like wattlebirds warbling, and it looks like flowers. It smells like flowers, too, which is nice for most people but not for people like Diana who have hay fever and get sniffly. Spring in Bloomsbury feels like sun, and it tastes like honeysuckle. I like spring because of my birthday, and because of school holidays. I don't like spring because it is swooping season, which means magpies are having babies and worrying about their babies and swooping anybody who walks near their babies. So even if you are just looking for peacocks or walking to school and have no intention of climbing a tree and stealing magpie babies you still have to look out for swooping magpie parents. The other reason I don't like spring is because it is snake-waking-up season, so you have to start stomping again when you walk in the bush.

And this spring I'm doing lots of bushwalking, because Jonas and I are looking for the peacocks again. We go out every day, with Simon and our backpacks and water and Irene's chocolate biscuits (which Jonas now agrees are just the right amount of chocolaty). We stomp hard, and we wear bike helmets with faces painted on the backs of them so the magpies won't swoop us. The peacock we see the most now is William Shakespeare. We see him the most because he has all his feathers again, so he is easy to spot. He is also doing a lot of dancing and singing, which makes him easy to find but hard to catch, because he is so busy and full of energy.

Then, yesterday, on the last day of the spring school holidays, The Peacock Detectives finally had a breakthrough.

"Wait a second," I said to Jonas, when we were walking on the track in the bush. I got my Notebook for Noticing out of my backpack and turned a lot of pages, all the way back to the day in March when the peacocks had escaped and I had gone into their cage to investigate. I reread what I had written:

Dirt scraped away
Trying to make a hole?

Then I looked back at the ground we were standing next to, where the dirt was scraped away, and the grass was dented.

"What is it?" Jonas said.

"Something," I said. I looked around. We were standing in the bush, but the bridge was only a few meters in front of us.

"Look!" I checked for cars and then ran onto the road. Jonas followed me. In the middle of the bridge, right on the white line, was something I had never seen before. But I knew straightaway—even before I felt its smooth, still-warm shape—what it was.

And what it was was a peacock egg.

Jonas went home to look up peacock eggs on the internet, and I took the egg straight to Mr. and Mrs. Hudson.

"They're making a nest!" I said, instead of "Hello" or "Good afternoon" or "Can I come in?"

Mrs. Hudson was sitting on the couch reading and Mr. Hudson was ironing a shirt. They both stopped what they were doing to look at the egg. It was a bit bigger than a chicken egg, and a bit more brown.

"It's definitely Virginia's," Mrs. Hudson said. "You can tell by the color."

I told her about the scratches in the ground, and how they were the same as the scratches I had seen in the peacock cage. "And it explains why Virginia was noisier than normal," I said, because I had just remembered how I had written down that detail without knowing why. Now I knew. "She was noisy about wanting to have babies!"

Then I told Mrs. Hudson that I had found the egg on the road. "It seems like a bad place to lay an egg to me," I said. "But I'm not a peacock."

Mrs. Hudson smiled. "It's a decoy egg," she said. "Peahens always lay one egg out in the open, to distract any predators from the rest of the clutch."

I stared at the decoy egg. It stared back at me, blank and silent. I thought about how brave this little egg was, sacrificing itself to save its brothers and sisters. "Will it hatch?" I asked.

Mrs. Hudson frowned. "It's unlikely," she said. "But if you take care of it and keep it warm enough, it might."

I looked up at her. "I can keep it?"

"Sure," Mrs. Hudson said. Then she looked at Mr. Hudson. "Cassie, if you find Virginia"—she looked back at me—"if she's with her nest, just leave her be. All right?"

I nodded. "Yes, Mrs. Hudson," I said.

As soon as the bell went at the end of school today Jonas and I went looking for Virginia's nest.

"We won't touch anything," I told Jonas as we walked toward the river. "We'll just have a look."

But we didn't get a chance to look. As soon as we got close to the bridge William Shakespeare appeared out of the bush. It was as if he was waiting for us. He had his tail open wide and he was squawking so loud I bet Mr. and Mrs. Hudson heard him from their house. When he knew that we had seen him he turned around and started running. On the bridge he stopped and looked back at us. He put his head on one side and squawked like he was saying "Hurry up!" (But I don't speak peacock, so he might have been saying "I like cheese.") I looked at Jonas, and Jonas looked at me. And then we did the only thing good Peacock Detectives can do in a situation like that. We chased William Shakespeare.

William Shakespeare isn't as fast as Virginia, but he is more confusing. He would run up one street, and then back down it again. He would fly over a fence or up a tree so we would think we had lost him, and then he would reappear and squawk at us to keep following. He ran past the hospital, and The Clinic, and the bus station. William Shakespeare ran us up and down and back and forth for ages, all over The Other Side of Town, until Jonas and I were both out of breath and had stitches. Then, finally, William Shakespeare flew into a clump of pine trees and didn't come out again. Jonas and I leaned against a tree trunk and slowly got our breath back. While we were leaning and breathing, Jonas saw something across the road. He squinted his eyes.

"Hey," he said, "is that—?"

"Rhea Grimm," I finished Jonas's sentence for him because he didn't have the breath for it. Rhea was walking along the side of the road on her own, scuffing her feet and stopping a lot to look at things or stare into the distance. From the way she walked and stopped and looked it was obvious she didn't want to get to the place she was going. I wanted to know where that place was.

"Let's follow her," I said.

"She's not a peacock," Jonas pointed out. "What about Virginia and the nest?"

I was starting to think there might be more to being a Peacock Detective than just finding peacocks. "We can look for them later," I said. "Come on."

So we followed Rhea, even though I could tell Jonas didn't really want to. Since that day on the basketball courts Jonas and I had avoided going to the secondary school at-all-costs. I think Jonas thought we should give up on Rhea completely, but I didn't want to. I still believed that there were two stories about her—one that was nice, and one that wasn't. I wanted the nice one to be the one people knew, and told, and wrote down.

We followed Rhea for a long time—partly because she was walking so slowly, and partly because where she was going was a long way from the bridge. It was so late in the afternoon that I was starting to worry about getting home to check on the egg. But then Rhea turned. And the place she turned at was Lee Street.

Jonas and I looked at each other, but didn't say anything. I could tell from Jonas's face that Irene had told him Lee Street was not the kind of place he should be hanging around, too. I could also tell that for him wanting to know what Rhea was doing was bigger than listening to his mum. So we kept following.

Lee Street was short, and it led to a dead end instead of another street. None of the houses had fences around their front yards, and the grass was long and full of weeds. The houses were faded like T-shirts that had been washed too many times, and the front windows were big and dark and made the houses look like they were hollow. There was stuff that should have been picked up all over the ground, like plastic buckets and chip packets and broken bike helmets. And it was really quiet. Even though it was the warm end of spring there were no kids playing outside, and no adults sitting on verandas drinking wine-before-dinner and chatting. The only sound was the buzz of TVs coming from behind closed doors and windows.

Rhea dawdled all the way to the dead end of the street, to a white house that wasn't exactly white anymore. Lots of the paint was peeling off like scabs, and the bits that weren't peeling had faded so they were the color of wet white dog.

Jonas and I hid across and up the street a bit, behind a tree. Part of me was scared to see Rhea walk into that house; I wanted to cover my eyes, like I did in the velociraptor bits of *Jurassic Park*. But then, before Rhea could get to the end of the path, the front door opened. And, instead of a monster or a velociraptor, a little girl with blond hair and a blue Dora the Explorer dress ran down the red bricks to meet Rhea. She looked about three years old and when Rhea picked her up the little girl smiled a smile that was almost bigger than her face.

Rhea twirled the little girl around in the air, and when she twirled in our direction Jonas and I saw that Rhea was smiling, too. Not just smiling—grinning. Not just grinning—*laughing*.

Jonas looked at me with a face that said, "Is that really Rhea Grimm?" And I looked back at him and said with (whispered) words: "See? I told you."

Because I was right. Rhea *was* a nice person (as well as sometimes a mean one). And—even though I didn't know exactly how I was going to do it—I knew I could make her be nice to us again, too.

THIRTY-FIVE

SINCE DAD DOESN'T LEAVE THE HOUSE ANYMORE, Diana and I do the shopping together. So today, I waited for Diana at the gate after school and we walked to the supermarket. My brain was still busy thinking about Rhea, so I didn't talk much. I wasn't sure whether Rhea would like me telling people about seeing her at the house on Lee Street. Something about it felt Personal—like taking a bus and a train to The City and not wanting to come back.

Diana didn't talk much, either. I wondered if her brain was busy with thinking about Buddhism, or Tom Golding, or something else that she didn't want to tell me about. I tried to guess what it might be, but now that

Diana is fifteen it is even harder for me to know what she is thinking.

We put the things from the shopping list into the cart quietly, and we only said things we needed to say, like "Pasta's in the next aisle" and "Do you want vanilla or strawberry yogurt?" By the time we had finished the cart was half-full with stuff for toasted cheese sandwiches and spaghetti, as well as other essentials like toilet paper and dishwashing liquid. We wobbled the cart on its slippery wheels over to the checkout and the woman scanned our items. Dollars added together on the little screen above the cash register. When everything was through and bagged and sitting neatly at the end of the checkout waiting for us to take it home, the woman said, "That's forty-six fifty, please."

Diana took Dad's credit card out of her bag and gave it to the woman.

"Tap?" The woman asked.

"Yes," Diana said.

The woman tapped the card against the machine. We waited. Diana twisted a piece of hair around her finger. This was strange because hair-twisting is usually something Mum does, not Diana.

After a minute the woman shook her head. "I'm sorry, sweetheart, it's been declined. Do you want me to try another card?"

Diana didn't say anything. She took a deep breath, and closed her eyes for a second. Then she just stood there, like she was frozen, staring at the woman and the card in her hand.

"What does declined mean?" I asked. The woman looked at me, then back at Diana. Still nobody said anything. And even though I didn't know what declined was I knew it wasn't good.

Finally, Diana said, "I'm sorry," to the woman and took the card back. Then she grabbed my hand and pulled me toward the exit. I turned around to look at our shopping sitting neatly on the counter.

"What about—" I started to ask, but Diana was already dragging me through the automatic doors. They opened and closed with a hiss.

"Just come on," she said, through gritted teeth. Gritting teeth is something Diana does when she is trying to keep in an emotion that wants to come out. She walked us all the way home like that, straight ahead and quickly, like she really needed to go to the toilet.

I found out which emotion Diana was keeping in as soon as we got home: an enormous amount of anger. Which was surprising, because usually Diana is calm and quiet and Buddhist. She released all of her anger right on top of Dad, who was sitting on the couch in his pajamas watching an after-school show about reptiles.

"Here," Diana yelled. She threw the declined card at Dad. It hit him in the middle of his chest and slid down to his stomach.

He stared at it like he had no idea what it was.

"So, now what?" Diana said this like she was spitting out chewing gum.

Dad didn't say anything.

"Well? What are we going to have for dinner?"

Diana was getting angrier each time she spoke. She started walking around, moving her arms and stomping her feet. She walked to the cupboard and opened it.

Then she started pulling out Dad's boxes.

"That could've been a loaf of bread," she said, opening a box and throwing a little gnome onto the floor. Then she threw a small piano at the wall. "That's two cartons of milk." A little monkey went flying. One of his hands broke off and rolled under the fridge. "A pack of toilet paper." A ceramic sandal. "Toothpaste." A fire truck. "Butter." The elephant skidded across the floor and slammed up against the TV cabinet. Its trunk broke off and lay on the lino, reaching for its body.

"I hope you're happy," Diana said, when she had emptied four boxes and the kitchen was full of broken ornaments. "I hope all of this made you really, really happy." She picked up her backpack and walked to the front door. "Come on, Cassie."

A big part of me wanted to go with her. A big part of me wanted to leave the messy kitchen that had nothing-for-dinner in it. But a bigger part was tugging me back. I looked at Dad's pajamas-face. I looked at the boxes, upside down and empty on the floor. And finally I looked at the little elephant whose trunk was broken. And even though I didn't really want to, I knew I had to stay.

I looked at Diana and shook my head. She made an angry humphing noise, kind of like a horse, and then she left.

After the door slammed I turned around to look at Dad. I was hoping to see something different about him. I was hoping that he had stood up, or crossed his legs, or at least stopped watching TV. But the only difference was that his eyes were glistening a little, like he almost-maybe-might-have wanted to cry.

THIRTY-SIX

NOW THAT IT'S NOVEMBER THE WEATHER IS almost warm enough for swimming. Jonas and I walk down to the river every day after school and stick our toes in.

"Almost," I say.

"But not quite," Jonas replies.

We still haven't found Virginia's nest, but we're not really trying that hard. We don't want to scare Virginia while she has eggs to sit on, and it's kind of fun chasing William Shakespeare all over town. I'm also busy with my decoy egg. Jonas read on the internet that peacock eggs need humidity to hatch, so we made an incubator out of some heat lamps and a box and a container of water. I sat it on my cupboard, and it's a lot of work rotating the egg and filling up the water when it evaporates.

After she *humphed* and left in October, Diana started living at Tom Golding's house. I know this because I see them walking to school together, and sometimes I see Mrs. Golding picking them up in the afternoons. Diana comes to see me in the primary school at lunchtimes. She gives me sandwiches and fruit and a juice box. "Go and stay at Mum's," she says, every day. Mum says this, too, when she comes over in the evenings with Tupperware containers of shepherd's pie and pumpkin soup. But I don't want to stay at Mum's. Partly because of Roger, but mostly because I can't imagine leaving Dad with only ornaments for company. I've tried, but I really can't imagine it.

For a while Dad and I didn't see each other very much. Dad was still in bed when I went to school in the mornings, and at night (after I heated up Mum's Tupperware dinner in the microwave) Dad went to his study and I went to my room to read or write. This worked because Dad didn't want to talk to me, and I had no idea what to say to Dad.

But then this morning I got chicken pox.

I used to not mind being sick—getting a bad cold, or a tummy bug, and not having to go to school. I like school most of the time, but I also like the way being sick makes things a little bit different for a while. Like when you change the furniture around in your room, or start wearing new socks.

But getting chicken pox meant being home. All day. With Dad. When I realized this I minded being sick. I minded a lot.

When I woke up this morning I knew something wasn't right. All my blankets and stuffed animals were on the floor, and usually they are snuggled around me until seven thirty. There were some strange grumblings in my stomach, but they weren't hunger-grumblings. I knew this was the start of being sick, but I pretended it wasn't. I got up and had a shower, even though the water felt like little needles going into my skin. I got dressed and put my schoolbooks in my bag, even though each time I moved, my stomach lurched like a boat in a bad storm.

I made some toast and put Vegemite on it, but no butter. I cut it into soldiers instead of triangles to delay the moment when I would have to put it in my mouth. When I picked up the first soldier my hand was shaking. I tried to talk myself into eating it:

"Wow, Cassie, this toast looks really delicious!"

"Bet you can't wait to take a bite!"

"Yum, toast! Just a few pieces and then off to school. I'm feeling great!"

And so on. I talked to myself until the toast went cold and the microwave clock said 8:45. I was about to be late. I took a big bite of the piece with the littlest scraping of Vegemite. I chewed. And swallowed. And ran to the toilet to throw up.

When Dad found me I was sitting-lying on the couch staring at my cold toast. The microwave clock said 9:36. Dad was still wearing his pajamas.

"School?" he asked when he saw me.

I swallowed some bad-tasting saliva and hugged my stomach, hoping I could push the urge to throw up again somewhere else. I couldn't.

"Going," I said, in one quick breath because breathing and talking at the same time was not good.

"Are you sick?"

"No," I breathed.

"Is it your tummy?"

"No." Speaking felt like trying to read a whole chapter book on a very bumpy bus ride up a very steep mountain.

"If you say so," Dad said. "Finish your breakfast, then, and I'll drive you." As soon as Dad pushed the toast toward me I lost all the control I had left. I threw up on the floor, and a little bit on Dad's slippers.

Dad carried me to my room. He put me in bed and picked up all my blankets and teddy bears. Then he went out and closed the door softly behind him. I fell asleep. Partly because there was nothing else to do, but mostly because I just couldn't help it.

When I woke up Dad was standing next to my bed. In one hand he had some flat lemonade and in the other he had a book.

"Is this what you're reading?" he asked. He gave the book to me. It was *I Capture the Castle* by Dodie Smith. I nodded. Then Dad gave me the lemonade and watched me drink half of it. I realized I was really thirsty. The lemonade wasn't as flat as Mum gets it, but it was still good.

"I'll come back in a little while," Dad said, and he turned toward the door.

"Wait!" I said, because I had just remembered. "The egg!"

Dad went over to my cupboard where the decoy egg was snuggled in its incubator. He picked it up. "It's fine," he said, "don't worry." He held the incubator carefully in two hands and left. I lay back on my pillows, and before I could wonder if I trusted Dad to keep my egg humid enough, I was asleep.

The next time I woke up it was late in the afternoon and I had little red chicken pox circles on my face and my tummy. Dad drove me to the doctor and the doctor said, "Yup, chicken pox."

"When can I go back to school?" I asked.

The doctor laughed. "Not for at least a week," she said. The word "week" rolled around in my brain like a ball in a pinball machine. A whole week without Jonas. A whole week without Diana. A whole week with Dad. The doctor must have seen vomit in my eyes, because she gave me a bucket before I could mess up her carpet.

We went home and I went back to bed. I read my book under the covers and slept. At teatime Dad brought me more flat lemonade and some dry toast. I ate two squares. I was about to fall asleep again when I heard Mum's voice.

"Possum! How are you feeling?" She was sitting on the edge of my bed touching my forehead.

"I'm fine, Mum," I said, because—apart from having chicken pox—I was.

"She's had her medicine, and some toast," Dad said, from my doorway. "She just needs to rest."

"I'll sit with her for a minute. Have you got something to read, Cassie?"

"Helen."

Mum turned around. Dad was looking at her with a face like a tree trunk—strong and solid. "I'll call you if we need anything," he said. Then he softened a bit. "I promise."

I could tell from the way Mum hugged me that she didn't want to leave, but she did anyway. I heard Mum and Dad talking in the kitchen for a while, then everything went quiet. Dad turned on the TV. I fell asleep again.

For two days I didn't do anything except sleep and drink flat lemonade and read-under-the-covers and try not to scratch myself. Then today, day three of having chicken pox, I started to feel a bit better. I woke up early and went into the kitchen for a change of scenery and maybe some breakfast. I was surprised to see Dad sitting at the kitchen table because he usually doesn't get up before nine thirty. He was wearing proper clothes, too: jeans, and a T-shirt that said "Surfers Paradise" and had a picture of a palm tree on the front, which he had bought on our Family Holiday. He even looked like he had had a shower.

On the table was one of the ornament boxes. Dad was staring into it, and even though he had proper clothes on he was still wearing his pajamas-face. When he saw me he smiled, but it was a smile that was covering a frown.

"Morning," he said. "Hungry?"

"A bit," I said.

"How about a scrape of jam this time?"

I nodded, and Dad got up to make my toast. I sat down at the table and looked into the box. The little elephant-without-a-trunk looked back at me.

When my toast was made, Dad sat at the table with me while I ate it. (I managed both pieces without the crusts.) When I was finished, the moment I had been dreading ever since I got chicken pox happened. Dad and I were alone, with no food or medicine or sleep between us. I took a deep breath and got ready for the long silence of Dad not wanting to talk, and me not knowing what to say.

But the silence didn't happen. And it didn't happen because Dad did have something to say, and what he said was: "Your grandma would've loved these."

He was looking into the box, so I knew he was talking about the elephant and the ceramic sandal and the monkey. I didn't know what to say. My grandma died when I was two years old, and I don't remember her. In photos she is a woman with curly hair and Dad's eyes and a nice smile. It didn't matter that I didn't say anything, though, because Dad wasn't finished talking.

"Our house was full of things like these, when I was small," he said. "On the windowsills, on top of the fireplace, even around the bathroom sink." Dad stopped for a moment and looked right at me, and in his eyes there wasn't happiness or sadness, but something in-between. "I used to make up stories about them," he said.

I put my hand into the box and pulled out the little elephant. I touched the empty place where her trunk had been. "Why do you keep them all in boxes?" I asked.

Dad looked surprised. For a moment he didn't answer, and then he said, "It's a bit weird, I guess."

"What's weird?"

He hesitated, and then pointed at the elephant in my hand. "Well, these."

I felt kind of insulted on behalf of the elephant, who had no way of sticking up for itself. "These aren't weird,"

I said. "Keeping them in the cupboard in boxes. That's weird."

Dad didn't reply. He wasn't wearing his pajamas-face, but he wasn't smiling, either. After the silence had gone on a bit too long he said, "You'd better go back to bed for a while."

I went, because I was still itchy and tired and a little bit queasy after the jam. When I got to the doorway and looked back at Dad he was wearing a face that I had never seen him wear. Before I fell asleep I hoped with all the hope in me that I hadn't said something that had broken him.

THIRTY-SEVEN

YESTERDAY—DAY FOUR OF HAVING CHICKEN POX—I WAS feeling okay enough to have a shower and wash my hair. When I walked into the kitchen with a towel on my head Dad was standing at the counter wearing his glasses and holding the little elephant and a tube of superglue.

"What are you doing?" I said.

Dad squirted a dollop of glue onto the elephant's face. "I thought I'd put it back together," he said. He placed the trunk carefully against the glue and held it there, firmly, for a minute. Then he put the elephant on top of the microwave. "What do you think?" he said.

I nodded. "It's happy up there," I said.

Dad poured me a glass of juice and made me toast

with jam and butter. While I was eating I thought about the story I had been trying to write. Before I got up to have a shower I had pulled my notebook and pen under the covers. But I was stuck. I only wrote two sentences before I gave up and went to wash my hair. And partly because I felt like the little elephant was telling me to, but mostly because I just really wanted someone to know, I decided to tell Dad the thing I had never told anyone before.

I pushed my empty plate out of the way and said, "Dad, I'm not sure I'm supposed to be a writer."

Dad picked up my plate and put it in the sink. "Why not?" he asked.

"Because sometimes writing is really hard."

Dad smiled. "Of course it is," he said.

"No." I put my hands flat on the table and made a triangle with my fingers. I didn't want to look at Dad when I told him this. "I mean, it's really, really hard. And sometimes I don't want to do it."

Dad didn't say anything for a while. He stared at the elephant on the microwave. Her superglued trunk was pointing straight up in the air. Then he said, "So why don't you stop?"

I thought about this. I imagined doing other things, instead of writing, like science experiments or cooking or javelin. But I realized none of these things would work.

And they wouldn't work because all the time in the back of my brain a voice is saying *WRITING WRITING WRITING*. If I try to clean my room: *WRITING WRIT-ING WRITING*. If I watch TV: *WRITING WRITING WRITING*. If I go for a walk with Simon each step I take says *WRI-TING WRI-TING WRI-TING*.

So I said to Dad, "Because I can't."

Dad pulled the monkey out of the box and put it on the windowsill. "Exactly," he said.

For the rest of the day each time I went into the kitchen there was another ornament somewhere. When I got up for a glass of water the bear was on the fridge. When I went to get a banana for lunch there was a small cat on the windowsill. And at dinnertime the little man was trimming his little roses on top of the television. Dad was standing in the middle of the kitchen with his hands on his hips. He looked like someone who had just finished writing a really good story.

Today was the last day of chicken pox (I wasn't itchy any-more and I could eat normal food in normal amounts). Dad woke me up early.

"Cassie, get up," he said. I followed him into the kitchen in my pajamas. When I had rubbed all the sleep out of my eyes I expected to see more ornaments. But that wasn't what Dad wanted to show me. He pushed me gently toward the couch. "Look," he whispered. And I looked.

And there, nestled between cushions and bits of fluff, was a sight so amazing I had to rub my eyes all over again to believe it. It squeaked, and wobbled, and still had bits of browner-than-chicken-eggshell stuck to its feathers. I looked at Dad. He smiled, and scooped the baby peacock carefully into his hand.

THIRTY-EIGHT

SUDDENLY IT IS SUMMER. SUMMER LOOKS LIKE bright blue skies and sounds like buzzing bees. Summer smells like cut grass, and tastes like popsicles, and feels like swimming in the river.

Being at home with Dad isn't so bad in summer. He hasn't gone back to work, but he has started wearing proper clothes every day, and making breakfast, and once a week he even goes shopping. He doesn't watch TV so much anymore, mostly because he is busy taking care of Leo (we decided to name the baby peacock after Leo Tolstoy, who is one of Dad's favorite writers). Leo needs a lot of taking care of. He has to be kept warm, and he has to drink a lot and eat a lot of green leafy things like cabbage and spinach. He also has to be picked up and held a lot so he knows that he is part of our family. Looking after Leo was supposed to be my job, since I had wanted to keep the decoy egg in the first place. But when Dad looks after Leo he has the same face as when he set up all his ornaments, so I decided he needs the job more than I do.

Every Friday afternoon Dad goes to The Clinic for an hour. When he comes home he is quiet, but not in the same way he is when he has Those Days. After The Clinic, Dad is quiet like Simon when he is sniffing, or like Diana when she is Meditating, or like Mum when she is cooking. It is a busy kind of quiet.

We go to visit Grandpa every afternoon, and I still have to sit in the hallway because Dad is still respecting-Mum's-wishes about me not seeing Grandpa Like That. But now instead of staring at the floor I read, or write a story.

Mum has started coming round more, but I can tell Dad doesn't really want her to. She isn't working as many nights at the restaurant anymore, so she has more time to cook us casseroles and lasagna and caramel slice. When she brings Tupperware containers Dad is very polite and says thank you but he doesn't invite her in for a cuppa.

In December we found Virginia's nest. Simon sniffed it out behind the bridge between a clump of blackberries and a wombat hole. There were five empty shells in it, and a lot of fluffy feathers that look exactly like Leo's.

But there was no sign of the babies, or Virginia. Even William Shakespeare has stopped playing chasey with us, although we can still hear him crying in the distance sometimes. His voice seems to be saying, "We're still here." But I don't speak peacock, so he might actually be saying, "Merry Christmas."

The beginning of summer means the end of school. We have stopped doing math and spelling and started making Christmas decorations and watching Christmas movies and practicing for the Christmas concert. We are practicing the same Christmas carols we sang last year, and the year before that. But this year they sound different because this is the last time we will ever sing them in primary school.

I think about Rhea a lot. The closer Christmas gets the more I think about Rhea and her house on Lee Street. Then today I had an idea.

Because Grandpa is in hospital we are having Christmas in our backyard this year, instead of at Aunt Sally's. Which means Dad and I are in charge of the Christmas list. Dad put on his glasses and I gave him a page from my Notebook for Noticing. First we wrote down Diana and Tom Golding. Then we wrote down Jonas and his parents, since Jonas's grandparents and aunties and uncles live far away. Then Dad said something that took me by surprise.

"We should invite your mum. And her friend."

I didn't say anything for a moment. Leo—who was standing on the table trying to help—pecked at my little finger. "We don't have to," I said. I knew one of the things Dad was doing to feel better was trying not to think about Mum.

"You should have your mum around for Christmas," Dad said. "I'm inviting them." And he wrote "Mum and friend" on the list. I think it was the hardest thing he has ever written.

Then I had my idea.

"Dad," I said. "Can I invite Rhea?"

Now it was Dad's turn to look surprised. "Rhea Grimm?"

I nodded.

"I didn't know you were friends with her."

"I'm not really."

Dad looked a little unsure, and maybe even a little scared. But he said, "All right, put her on the list."

And I wrote Rhea's name.

When I told Jonas about inviting Rhea to Christmas he was skeptical. Skeptical means you don't completely believe in something, like when someone tells you Brussels sprouts are good for you.

"Why would she want to have Christmas with us?" he said. "She hates us."

"Don't worry," I said. "I have a plan."

So today after school instead of looking for the peacocks, Jonas and I looked for Rhea. We found her on the other side of the bridge, dawdling along the road on her way home to Lee Street. When I spotted her I took a deep breath. And then I yelled, "Rhea! Wait!"

She turned around. I could tell from her stiff, straight shape that she wasn't happy to see us. I ran across the bridge. Jonas walked. Slowly.

"What do you want?" Rhea said when I got close to her. Her voice was a mixture of angry and sighing.

"I just wanted . . . I was wondering . . ." Now that I was close to Rhea and could see how tall she was, and how jangly her bangles were, and how unhappy her face was I started to feel unsure of my plan. I looked down at my shoes and said in one long shaky breath, "Do-you-want-to-come-to-my-house-for-Christmas?"

I could feel Jonas behind me getting ready to run back across the bridge. When I looked up Rhea was staring at me the way people stare at bungee jumpers—half annoyed at their stupidity, and half impressed by it. She shook her head and turned away.

"Wait," I said. Behind me I could feel Jonas thinking I had really lost it. Rhea waited. "You were right," I said. "You were right about my dad."

Rhea turned around. Her face shifted slightly, like a bike changing gears.

"My dad *is* crazy," I said. And saying it felt like pushing a boulder to the top of a mountain. "He talks to himself. He doesn't go to work. Sometimes he sits and stares at the living room wall for an hour without moving. He hardly eats. He spent all his money on ornaments. My mum doesn't want to live with him anymore. My sister moved out, too." I looked down at my hands. They were shaking. "Anyway." I looked back at Rhea. "I just thought you should know. You were right."

Rhea stared at me for a long time. For a moment I thought she was going to say something, but then she turned around and started walking away. Jonas put his hand on my arm.

"Let's go," he said.

I shook my head. I didn't want to go home. I didn't want to go anywhere.

"I'm going to stay here for a while," I said. I could tell Jonas understood because he didn't try to change my mind. He nodded, and then he walked back across the bridge.

I didn't know what else to do, so I picked up a stick and threw it into the river. Then I walked to the other side of the bridge and watched it come out. I picked up another stick and threw it. Walked. Watched. Picked up another stick. Walked. Watched. Picked up another stick. I don't know how long I did this for, or how many times, because while I was doing it I stopped thinking about time or Dad or Rhea or peacocks. I was only thinking about sticks and walking and watching.

When I saw two sticks come out from under the bridge instead of one I expected to see Diana standing on the other side of the road. But when I looked it wasn't Diana. It was Rhea Grimm.

When Rhea walked over to look at her stick (which was a little bit slower than mine) she said, "Does your dad really do all those things?"

"Cross my heart," I said.

There was a long pause while we watched our sticks disappear down the river. When we couldn't see them anymore Rhea said, "My dad used to stare at the wall, too."

We walked back to get two more sticks and then we threw them off the bridge. This time Rhea's was faster. Without looking at me, she said, "Christmas lunch, or Christmas dinner?"

"Lunch," I said. Rhea nodded.

We kept playing Pooh Sticks until it got late. I told Rhea about how my dad knows a lot about stories, and she told me how her dad is really good at tennis. And even though we didn't say it, I knew we were both thinking how weird it was that dads could be so crazy and so cool at the same time.

THIRTY-NINE

ON CHRISTMAS MORNING, DAD WOKE ME UP at seven o'clock and we went out onto the deck. Simon was sitting in front of the Christmas tree watching Leo, who is much bigger now and has most of his proper feathers. He can even fly a little bit, which is upsetting to Simon because flying is something he will never be able to do. Apart from Leo's flapping and landing, Christmas morning was really still and quiet. I thought about how Aunt Sally's house sounds on Christmas: there are kids yelling, and Christmas music, and dogs barking, and pancakes hissing on the stove. I love Christmas at Aunt Sally's, but there was something nicely different about Christmas in my own backyard.

As I looked around with sleepy seven-a.m. eyes it felt like I was seeing everything for the first time. The chestnut tree with its big spreading arms, the long grass full of bugs, the rosebushes climbing along the back fence. Diana's tent wasn't there anymore, now that she was living at Tom Golding's. I missed it, and I missed her, but I understood now why she was gone.

The yard all felt somehow new and fresh and different, even though it was all exactly the same as it had always been. On Christmas morning in my backyard I only needed exactly what I already had. And then I realized—not suddenly and surprisingly, but slowly and quietly—that I did know what Buddhism was. It wasn't about not needing anything—Buddhism was about not needing anything *else*.

For a Christmas present Dad gave me a new notebook with a picture of a peacock on the cover. It is the best notebook I have ever owned. I felt bad because Dad's Christmas present from me was supposed to be this story, but it isn't finished yet.

"I thought it would be finished by now," I said. "But it doesn't have an ending."

"Don't worry," Dad said. "The ending will come when it's ready."

After church we set up the backyard for Christmas lunch. We pushed plastic tables together on the grass under the chestnut tree and covered them with Christmas tablecloths so you couldn't see the wobbly joints in the middle. Dad got the barbecue ready and I put the cutlery and napkins on the tables. Simon and Leo were wearing their Christmas ribbons, Dad was wearing his good shirt, and I was wearing the new dress Aunt Sally had sent me for Christmas (which is green and blue and has a matching belt). We were ready.

I was really hoping Mum and Roger wouldn't arrive first, but they did.

"Merry Christmas, possum!" Mum bent down to kiss me and then went straight into the kitchen. Roger followed her, balancing lots of Tupperware containers in his arms. Mum pulled an apron out of the bottom drawer and turned on the oven. When Dad came inside and saw Mum holding a tray of glazed pumpkin he didn't look happy.

"Helen, I've already cooked," he said, which was true. Dad had spent most of Christmas Eve in the kitchen, swearing a lot and spilling things, but by the end of it the fridge was full of Christmas food.

"It's fine," Mum said. "It just means we'll have a few leftovers."

Dad frowned. I could tell he knew whose food would end up being left over. I was worried for a minute that Mum and Dad were about to have a fight, but then Diana and Tom Golding arrived, so they couldn't. Dad said hello to Diana, and shook Tom's hand. I could tell Diana was surprised to see Dad wearing his good clothes and greeting people.

Mum started heating some oil in a frying pan, and Dad mumbled something about the barbecue and disappeared outside. Roger opened a bottle of wine and poured some into a glass. He put his arm around Mum's shoulders.

"Well," he said, "should we have a Christmas toast?" He pulled Mum close to him. I got ready to run outside before something disgusting happened. But something surprising happened instead. Mum pushed Roger away.

"I'm trying to do the spring rolls," she said. Roger took his arm back. He stood in the middle of the kitchen like he didn't know what to do. For a moment the only sound was hot oil popping and sizzling.

Then a second surprising thing happened. Diana said, "Can I do anything?" And she went and stood next to Mum.

All of this behavior was very confusing, so I was relieved when there was another knock at the door. It was Jonas and his parents.

"Merry Christmas!" Peter said.

"Merry Christmas!" Irene said.

"Did you know starlight is four years old before we see it?" Jonas said.

Jonas and I went outside to see Leo and Simon, and

to give each other presents. I gave Jonas my copy of *The Hound of the Baskervilles*, and he gave me a book called *Believe It or Not: Science Facts!* I was reading a science fact about monkfish when Dad came over with the tongs.

"I'm going to turn on the barbecue," he said. "Is everyone here?"

Diana and Tom Golding were sitting at the wobbly Christmas tables. Mum was with the spring rolls. Roger was on the couch with a glass of wine.

"Rhea's not," Jonas said.

Dad looked at me and said, "Then you'd better go and find her."

FORTY

JONAS AND I LEFT THE CHRISTMAS LUNCH and went out onto the Christmas streets. I held Simon's lead and Leo walked-flapped beside us. Diana and Tom Golding came too, except they walked so far behind that they might as well not have been there at all. Everything shimmered in the heat like it didn't really exist. There was nobody else around—no cars, and no pedestrians. Everyone was at home eating Christmas lunch or playing Christmas charades. Walking through Christmas-Bloomsbury was like walking through a ghost town.

It took more than half an hour to get to Lee Street—partly because it's really far away, but mostly because Diana and Tom Golding were walking so slowly. The street was deserted, and the only sound was the hum of TVs from inside the houses. Walking along Lee Street was like walking into a beehive.

We walked along the brick path to Rhea's front door. From the porch of Rhea's house the street looked surprisingly different—like a street that led somewhere, and not like a dead end. I knocked.

There was silence for a long time. My ears felt like they were stretching off the sides of my head, trying to hear something—anything—from inside the house. But there was nothing. I knocked again. This time there was the sound of feet running on carpet, and the door opened.

At first I thought there was no one there. Then I looked down. A little boy with messy hair and red cheeks was standing in the doorway.

"Hi," he said.

"Hi," I said. "What's your name?"

He rubbed one of his cheeks. There was something sticky on his hand, and it came off just under his eye. "I'm not allowed to talk to strangers," he said. "Are you strangers?"

I knelt down so I wasn't taller than him anymore. "My name's Cassie," I said. "And this is Jonas. And that's"—I turned around and pointed to where Diana and Tom Golding were dawdling down Lee Street—"my sister and a boy who is her friend, but not her boyfriend."

The little boy's eyes went wide. "You're the Peacock Detectives!"

I felt my face go red.

"I'm Felix," the little boy said, and he led us through the house, which was much nicer on the inside than it was on the outside. Rhea was in the kitchen surrounded by pots and pans and flour and a big mess. Her face was red and her hair was stuck to her forehead with sweat. When she saw us her face turned even redder.

"What are you doing here?" she said.

"We've come to get you," I said. I looked around the kitchen. "What are you doing?"

"We're making turkey and stuffing and pudding and custard," Felix said. I realized the smudge of sticky under his eye was cranberry sauce. "Mum had to go to work so Rhea's in charge."

Rhea made a face like a squashed frog. "It's chicken, Felix, not turkey," she said. "And I think the custard's gone off."

"How many brothers and sisters do you have?" said Diana. She had finally made it into the kitchen. Tom Golding was right beside her.

"Five," Felix said. "Me, and Rhea, and Ada, and Paige, and Henry. Rhea's the oldest, and then Henry. He's nine."

"Why don't you come to our place?" Diana said. "We've got way too much food anyway."

Rhea looked at Diana, and then at the sticky counters, and then at me. Part of her look was angry, but another, larger part was very, very tired.

Before the angry part of Rhea could tell us to go away, Felix noticed Leo, who was flapping his wings behind Tom Golding. "Is that a *peacock*?" he said, and before I could blink Felix was holding Leo in his arms.

I looked at Rhea.

She sighed. "Fine," she said. "Let's go, then."

So seven kids, two teenagers, one peacock chick, and one Brittany spaniel started walking back down Lee Street toward the river. We weren't looking for anything except Christmas lunch, so when Felix started jumping and pointing I thought he was going crazy from hunger. But then I looked, and I saw what he was jumping and pointing at. And what he was pointing at was William Shakespeare and Virginia.

They were on the bridge. At first I thought the shimmery heat was playing tricks on my eyes, but then I heard them. They called out to each other in that long, sad peacock voice that sounds like something is dying and being saved at the same time.

Leo heard it too, and started chirping. I picked him up and held him carefully. Then I turned around and pressed a finger to my lips. Jonas and Rhea nodded. All of Rhea's brothers and sisters went very still and didn't make a sound.

The peacocks were strutting right down the middle of the road with their heads held high, as proud as peacocks. I suppose they thought they would be safe, since it was Christmas and everyone was at home having Christmas lunch. William Shakespeare was in front, letting his tail trail lazily behind him. Virginia was at the back, and in between them were five feathery, flapping peacock chicks.

We moved quickly and quietly off the road and into the bush. We crept crouched-down toward the bridge, careful not to crunch any loud sticks with our shoes. Jonas and Rhea were right behind me with Simon, and Diana and Tom Golding were behind the little kids. The kids didn't giggle or talk or play. They were Peacock Detectives now, too.

When we got to the bridge we stopped and waited by the riverbank at the edge of the road. The peacocks had stopped as well. There was a long moment where nothing happened, and the only sound was thousands of summer cicadas. Then William Shakespeare poked his head over the side of the bridge. Leo started chirping, and Simon started barking.

And The Peacock Detectives charged.

The peacocks saw us coming and started to run. But there were more of us, and we spread out and surrounded them. Jonas cornered Virginia against the side of the bridge and was bravely approaching her. But she lunged forward and pecked at him, and Jonas jumped out of the way. Virginia turned and ran in the opposite direction—right into Tom Golding.

"I've got her!" Tom Golding shouted. He had his arms wrapped gently but firmly around Virginia's wings. When the peacock chicks saw that their mum had been captured they ran toward her. Felix picked one up, Henry got another one, and so did Ada. Even Paige had a chick cuddled in her arms.

William Shakespeare, however, was getting away.

"Take them home!" I yelled to Diana, who was staring at Tom Golding like she had never seen him before. She nodded and they went. I held Leo—who was still chirping—against me. Then Rhea, Jonas, Simon, and I chased William Shakespeare.

I had never seen a peacock run so fast before. It must have been the open roads. Out in the empty space of Christmas afternoon William Shakespeare had room to run. And he really ran. His feet sped across the hot asphalt in a blur. Jonas and Simon were close behind him, but I could tell Jonas was getting tired. He started to slow down, and for a moment I thought we were going to lose William Shakespeare. But then Rhea lunged ahead and almost caught his tail. William Shakespeare must have felt the breeze of Rhea's hand against his feathers, because he picked up more speed. He ran straight up the hill, and past the church. And through the gates of the school.

The playground was just as empty as the rest of town. William Shakespeare darted past the music room, and for a second I thought he was going to keep going straight across the handball courts and into the secondary school. But at the last minute he veered right. He was going so fast that when he turned he almost fell over. He was trying to outwit us. He ran with his feathers tucked behind him so his body was shaped like a rocket. He kept twisting and turning and pretending to go in one direction, then choosing another. We zigged and zagged all over the school. Then suddenly William Shakespeare made a quick right turn—toward The Snake Stairs.

By now Rhea and Jonas were out of breath and I was in the lead. I was running so fast and I was so focused on William Shakespeare's tail that I completely forgot I'm scared of snakes and that I never go past the edge of the footpath. By the time I remembered these things it was too late—I was at the bottom of the stairs.

I had forgotten to stomp.

And the tiger snake was rearing up at me.

I've heard stories about snakes hypnotising people, and I never really believed them. But at that moment, staring at the tiger snake breathing and lifting and flattening itself out in front of me, I was hypnotized. The top of its body was a shiny black, as dark as space. Its tummy was a clean bright yellow, the color of spring wattle. It was hissing and the top part of its body was puffed up like a balloon. I could see its forked tongue flicking. Its eyes were open and looking. And they were looking straight at me.

While the snake was looking at me I was surprised by two things:

1. That it was beautiful, and
2. I didn't stomp, or scream, or try to run away. I just stood there—like Jonas had when he saw the snake near the river behind his house—and did nothing.

The tiger snake moved its head back and then forward. I knew—the way I know that two plus two is four and that Simon loves bones—that the snake was about to bite me. I closed my eyes and prepared to be bitten.

Suddenly there was a piercing squawk that broke my hypnosis and almost burst my eardrums.

William Shakespeare ran between me and the tiger snake. He opened his tail like a shield and shook his eye-feathers, so he looked like a tree rustling in a breeze. William Shakespeare's head was level with the snake's head, and he bobbed it like he was getting ready to attack.

The snake hissed again and tried to strike at William Shakespeare's legs, but William Shakespeare was too fast. He moved back and then forward straightaway, and pecked the end of the tiger snake's tail. The snake pulled its head down and looked around, like it was thinking about what to do next. It looked at all of us one by one with both eyes—Rhea, Jonas, Simon, me, Leo, and William Shakespeare. And the look in the snake's eyes was frightening, but it was also frightened. It gave one last hiss, and then dropped to the ground and slid back under The Snake Stairs.

For a moment no one did anything. Then Simon barked and Leo chirped. And when I put my arms around William Shakespeare I was partly catching him, but I was mostly giving him a hug.

FORTY-ONE

EVERY STORY HAS A CLIMAX. THE CLIMAX is the part when the problem from the beginning of the story—the Inciting Incident—is finally solved. A lot of things have happened already in this story, like Jonas running away and Diana moving outside and Leo hatching. But the Climax didn't happen until today, when we caught the peacocks.

Maybe you were expecting the Climax to be more exciting. Maybe you were hoping someone would get bitten by the tiger snake, so they would have to go to hospital in an ambulance and there would be sirens and doctors and people crying. But Climaxes aren't always big and noisy and dramatic. Sometimes they are quiet, like a snake sliding under some stairs.

When we got home Rhea's brothers and sisters had finished eating Christmas lunch and were playing cricket. We took William Shakespeare across the road to the vacation flats, and Virginia and the peacock chicks were very happy to see him. Mr. and Mrs. Hudson were happy, too, but in a less squawky way.

Mrs. Hudson gave Rhea, Jonas, and me twenty dollars and a box of biscuits for being excellent Peacock Detectives, and we went back across the road to see what was left of Christmas lunch. There turned out to be a lot—the fridge was still half full of Dad's and Mum's cooking. Mum had even made lemon meringue pie—which is my favorite dessert—with whipped cream and without glazed pomegranate peel or cherry-crusted cashews. While I was eating Mum told me she wasn't going to be working at The Very Nice Restaurant anymore.

"Why not?" I asked. Except I had a mouthful of lemon meringue, so it sounded more like "I ot?"

"It wasn't really for me," Mum said. She said she was looking for another job. She was still going to be living in The Flat, though. When I asked where Roger was, Mum looked over at Dad, who was washing the dishes. "He couldn't stay," was all she said.

When the kids had finished playing cricket (Felix got twelve runs and told everybody about it twelve times) they came inside and Dad opened up the rest of his cardboard boxes and handed out ornaments to everyone. And Rhea's brothers and sisters didn't think having boxes full of ornaments was weird at all. I looked carefully at Dad's face to make sure he wasn't too sad to say goodbye to all the little things he had bought. He did look a little sad, but not in a Those Days way. When he caught me staring at him he said, "Don't worry, I'm keeping the elephant."

It got late in the afternoon, and Jonas went home with his parents. ("Did you know this was the best Christmas ever?" he said as they went out the door. Which I thought was a weird thing to say, since I had almost been bitten by a snake.) Rhea's mum came to pick up her family and when everyone was introducing themselves a strange and amazing thing happened.

"I'm Diana," Diana said. "And this is Tom. My boyfriend."

Nobody knew what to say, except Rhea's mum, who didn't know anyone and certainly didn't know who was supposed to be whose boyfriend and who wasn't. And Rhea's mum said, "Nice to meet you, Tom," which was exactly right.

Then it was four o'clock, and everyone was gone except my family. And that meant it was time to go to the hospital to visit Grandpa.

When we got there I sat down in the hallway like always and got ready to imagine more horrible Grandpas that I would still want to see. But then Dad said, "Cassie, do you want to come in?"

I blinked at him a few times, because I wasn't sure I had heard him right. I wondered for a moment if William Shakespeare *had* damaged my eardrums with his heroic squawk.

"Yes," I said, because I did want to come in, and I had ever since the end of autumn.

Dad looked at Mum, but in a different way from usual. Usually when Dad looks at Mum his face is like a big question mark, like all of his features are saying, "Is that okay?" But this time he looked at her with a face like a full stop. Like all of him was saying, "That's what I think should happen."

I thought Mum was definitely going to argue with Dad, but she didn't. Instead she looked at him with a face like a semicolon; open and unfinished. Then she said, "Come on, Cassie."

And we all walked through the door together.

It was a nice room. There was a big window at the back, and the late afternoon sun was coming in and crawling across the floor. The tips of the sun's fingers touched the end of a long white bed. In the bed was Grandpa.

I studied him carefully, from his feet up to his head. His legs were under the sheet. They looked a bit skinny, but they didn't seem to have any spikes or bumps or extra toes. He was wearing pajamas with short sleeves and his arms came out of them like sticks. But they were still his arms. They had the same knobbly elbows as before, the same hairs, the same brown spots on the backs of their hands. The little crease between his neck and his chest seemed deeper than usual, and the skin under his chin was a bit looser. His cheeks were more sucked in, his chin was pointier, and his forehead seemed higher. The top of his head was shinier. But it was still his head. It was still his face. He hadn't turned into a skeleton, or a vampire, or a monster, or anything else my brain had imagined while I was sitting in the hallway. He was still my grandpa.

For a minute I stood by the bed watching Grandpa breathe in and out. Then he opened his eyes. They were the same deep, clear blue that they had always been. They were staring at me now, ready to hear whatever I wanted to say.

I unzipped my backpack and Leo poked his head out. He was smart enough not to chirp too loudly. I showed him to Grandpa.

"Hi, Grandpa," I said. "Can I tell you a story?"

He nodded. So I did.

FORTY-TWO

GRANDPA DIED ON THE 3RD OF JANUARY. It was the middle of the afternoon and I was swimming in the river with Jonas when Dad came to tell me. At the funeral Diana and I sat next to each other, and Mum and Dad held hands.

We were all crying, and even though I know it sounds weird something about us all being there together felt like our Family Holiday, which was a feeling I thought I would never feel again. Whenever I remember our Family Holiday now it is a mix of good and bad. I remember how Diana played in the pool with me some days, and how it rained on others. And I remember how Mum and Dad argued about where to go for dinner, and also how they teased each other about Scrabble words.

Three weeks after the funeral I walked across the handball courts and started secondary school. It was a bit scary, but not the kind of scary that comes from being in a really dangerous situation. More like the kind of scary that comes from watching *Jurassic Park*, which is scary mixed with exciting and interesting. My favorite thing about secondary school is being allowed to take books out from the teenage section of the library. Jonas's favorite thing about secondary school is using Bunsen burners in science (which I also think is pretty cool).

Even though we're not in primary school anymore Jonas and I still eat our lunch on The Snake Stairs. I don't sit on the other side of the footpath anymore. I sit right up on the top step, next to Jonas.

I see Rhea on the basketball courts sometimes. We're not really friends, but we're not enemies, either, which is a good start. She is still tired and grumpy a lot because she has to spend her after-school time taking care of her brothers and sisters. But she is trying harder at school, and Rhea's mum says that in a few weeks she will take time off work so she and Rhea can go to The City to visit Rhea's dad. Rhea never told me what her Personal reason for running away was, but I think I know. Like Jonas, Rhea was looking for someone who couldn't be found.

Jonas still complains about his parents, but now he complains about them like they are really his parents, and not just strangers he has to live with. He gets annoyed when his mum wants to walk to school with him, and when she puts notes in his lunch box that say things like "Did you know your dad and I love you very much?" He crumples them up, but he never throws them in the bin.

Diana is in Year Ten now, which means she has a lot more math assignments to do, which she loves. Her boyfriend, Tom, doesn't understand math, but Diana is really good at helping him. Diana still Meditates, and two weeks ago she moved back home, so now she does it in our backyard. She doesn't mind if I want to sit next to her and do it, too. When I told her I had figured out what Buddhism really meant, she smiled at me and said, "Me too," which didn't make sense to me, because I thought she had known what it was all along.

Mr. and Mrs. Hudson decided that the peacocks didn't want to be ornamental after all. They found a wildlife park for William Shakespeare and Virginia to live in where they have lots of space to roam and have more babies. I asked Mrs. Hudson if she thought I should send Leo to the wildlife park, too, but she said it was pretty clear that Leo was happy with us. I breathed an inside sigh of relief when she said that. I would really miss Leo if he wanted to go to the wildlife park, and I think Dad would miss him even more.

Mum and Dad aren't back together, and Mum is still

living in The Flat on The Other Side of Town. But she comes to visit a lot, and we have family dinner once a week. She got a job at a new bakery that opened in the Bloomsbury main street. They make lots of delicious things like cinnamon rolls and vanilla slices and custard tarts. Mum's lemon meringue pie is the bakery's best seller.

I can tell Dad still misses Mum because of the way he smiles when her car pulls into our driveway every Friday night. But he is trying really hard not to be sad. He gets up early most mornings, and buys groceries and cooks dinner and takes Simon and Leo for walks. He still has Those Days, but not as much anymore. I told Dad how I sometimes have Those Days, too, and it made him smile a bit to know that this is another thing that makes us the same. He said sometimes talking about Those Days makes them easier to get through, and that I can tell him anything, any time. I already knew this, but it made me happy to hear him say it out loud. In January, Dad went back to work, and he even started writing stories again. He spends a lot of time with Leo, who—even though he is big now—likes to sit under Dad's desk in his study while he is working.

I still don't know if this story has Themes in it. Maybe you can find some. I know I said at the beginning that this was a story about peacocks, but that turned out to be not completely true. And it wasn't completely true because—even though I didn't know it at the time—this story is actually about lots of things. Which is kind of what life is like. When I realized this I decided to change my equation. Now it looks like this:

Cassie = Peacock Detective

Which doesn't just mean I'm someone who looks for peacocks. It also means I'm someone who writes stories, and someone who reads, and someone who is a sister, and a daughter, and a friend, and a dog-walker, and a Year Seven student, etc etc etc. It is a list that can go on forever, and can always be added to.

But even though the list is never-ending, every story has to end somewhere.

Today at lunchtime when we were sitting on The Snake Stairs Jonas said, "Did you know you've been writing that story for almost a year?"

"Yes," I said. "But I'm going to finish it now."

"Why now?" Jonas asked.

"Partly because Christmas was ages ago and it's Dad's Christmas present," I said. "And partly because the peacocks aren't escaped anymore. But mostly because when this story is finished I can start a new one."

"What will it be about?"

"I don't know," I said.

"Then how will you start it?"

I looked down through the gaps between The Snake Stairs. "I'll just write down everything I can," I said, "until I find a story." And I knew I would. Cross my heart.

ACKNOWLEDGMENTS

THE PEACOCK DETECTIVES COULD NOT HAVE BEEN written without a lot of help. I'd like to say a huge thank you to the following people. To those readers of early drafts and givers of thoughtful feedback: Luke Young, Loralie Young, Natalie Jane Peou, John Christopher Brown, James Christy, Claire Marchant-Collier, Jehangir Mehentee, Bryan Humphrey, Abby Millerd, Kathryn Whinney, Chris Sanders, Monique Hutchinson, Michelle St. George, Marije Klijn, and everyone from Seoul Writers Workshop and Phnom Penh Writers Workshop.

To Ella MacDermott, for her insightful review—I know Cassie would love to be your friend. To Lin Kim, for reading and for helping me remember why writing is so important. To Tee O'Neill, for being the best mentor I could ever ask for.

To my best friend, Emma Manning, for her beautiful drawings and her songs. To Peta Cherry for coffee and books. To Georgia Brown for long chats and cats. To Vanessa Danielsen, Erica Hamence, and Avalon Carr for Skype dates and live feeds.

To Robyn and Greg Schultz and all the wonderful staff at Riverdeck Café in Bright, for giving me a job, a place to write, and cake.

To the students and staff at Porepunkah Primary School, for their love of reading and for reminding me just how important books are.

To Nannie, for sharing novels and scone recipes. To Apam and Panda, for homemade pasta and ideas about passata. To my brother, Bradley, for making lists and helping me tick them off. And to Mum and Dad, for their constant support and encouragement.

To everyone at Text Publishing, for their enthusiasm for *The Peacock Detectives*. And especially to Jane Pearson, whose meticulous editing helped make this book the best it could be.

To Jake, for having a great sense of smell. And to Penny, for all the licks.

Finally, to Andrew. I love you.